Her whispered plea was a tantalizing caress in the intimacy of the night. But temptation had never been this seductive. Need had never been this great.

Fighting both, he made himself take that step.

The rustle of bedclothes, the softness of her fingers at his wrist, stopped his movements and his heartbeat. She didn't say a word—she didn't have to.

Without turning to face her, he let out a ragged breath, shook his head. "This isn't smart, Maddie."

Her reply, when it finally came, was sunrise soft but as inevitable as nightfall. "You think I don't know that?"

He turned to face her. "Then why?"

The eyes that met his were swimming with confusion, and wonder, and need. "I don't know. I don't want to know. I just want...just please... don't go."

Dear Reader,

All of us at Silhouette Desire send you our best wishes for a joyful holiday season. December brings six original, deeply touching love stories warm enough to melt your heart!

This month, bestselling author Cait London continues her beloved miniseries THE TALLCHIEFS with the story of MAN OF THE MONTH Nick Palladin in *The Perfect Fit*. This corporate cowboy's attempt to escape his family's matchmaking has him escorting a *Tallchief* down the aisle. Silhouette Desire welcomes the cross-line continuity FOLLOW THAT BABY to the line with Elizabeth Bevarly's *The Sheriff and the Impostor Bride*. And those irresistible bad-boy James brothers return in Cindy Gerard's *Marriage, Outlaw Style*, part of the OUTLAW HEARTS miniseries. When a headstrong bachelor and his brassy-but-beautiful childhood rival get stranded, they wind up in a 6lb., 12oz. bundle of trouble!

Talented author Susan Crosby's third book in THE LONE WOLVES miniseries, *His Ultimate Temptation*, will entrance you with this hero's primitive, unyielding desire to protect his once-wife and their willful daughter. A rich playboy sweeps a sensible heroine from her humdrum life in Shawna Delacorte's Cinderella story, *The Millionaire's Christmas Wish*. And Eileen Wilks weaves an emotional, edge-of-your-seat drama about a fierce cop and the delicate lady who poses as his newlywed bride in *Just a Little Bit Married?*

These poignant, sensuous books fill any Christmas stocking—and every reader's heart with the glow of holiday romance. Enjoy!

Best regards,

Joan Marlow Golan
Senior Editor

Please address questions and book requests to:
Silhouette Reader Service
U.S.: 3010 Walden Ave., P.O. Box 1325, Buffalo, NY 14269
Canadian: P.O. Box 609, Fort Erie, Ont. L2A 5X3

MARRIAGE, OUTLAW STYLE
CINDY GERARD

SILHOUETTE *Desire*
Published by Silhouette Books
America's Publisher of Contemporary Romance

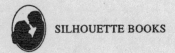

SILHOUETTE BOOKS

ISBN 0-373-76185-6

MARRIAGE, OUTLAW STYLE

Printed in U.S.A.

Books by Cindy Gerard

Silhouette Desire

The Cowboy Takes a Lady #957
Lucas: The Loner #975
*The Bride Wore Blue #1012
*A Bride for Abel Greene #1052
*A Bride for Crimson Falls #1076
‡The Outlaw's Wife #1175
‡Marriage, Outlaw Style #1185

*Northern Lights Brides
‡Outlaw Hearts

CINDY GERARD

If asked "What's your idea of heaven?" Cindy Gerard would say a warm sun, a cool breeze, pan pizza and a good book. If she had to settle for one of the four, she'd opt for the book, with the pizza running a close second. Inspired by the pleasure she's received from the books she's read and her longtime love affair with her husband, Tom, Cindy now creates her own warm, evocative stories about compelling characters and complex relationships.

All that reading must have paid off, because since winning the Waldenbooks Award for Best Selling Series Romance for a First-Time Author, Cindy has gone on to win the prestigious Colorado Romance Writers' Award of Excellence, *Romantic Times Magazine* W.I.S.H. Awards, Career Achievement and Reviewers' Choice nominations, and the Romance Writers of America's RITA nomination for Best Short Contemporary Romance.

This book is dedicated to free spirits
and the fun and excitement they bring to our lives.

Prologue

Women had always held Clay James's interest. They amused him. Sometimes they amazed him. Regularly they aroused him. But no woman had ever rubbed him in all the wrong ways like Maddie Brannigan.

With a smug sort of satisfaction, Clay watched Maddie cross his brother Garrett's backyard, a cold can of soda in her hand. He thumbed back his tan Stetson, hooked a thumb in the belt loop of his pressed denims and spared a moment to pity Joe Banyon, the poor schmuck who was putting up with her lip today.

The party was in full swing. The whole family, as well as a bevy of friends, were celebrating Garrett and Emma's eleventh wedding anniversary. The two of them had experienced some rocky times recently. You'd never know it to look at them now, but it had gotten so rough that Emma had actually left Garrett a few months ago. With a wry grin, Clay remembered his part in the kidnapping the James boys had staged to help get the two of them back together.

Fortunately it had all worked out, and the brothers hadn't ended up in jail like their notorious outlaw ancestors—although at one point in time some would have argued that the population of Jackson Hole would sleep better at night if the James boys were out of circulation.

Clay agreed that may have been a valid concern once, but Maya James Bradford's boys had mellowed some over the years. Especially Garrett. Clay watched with a smile as Garrett held eight-year-old Sara on his hip and pulled Emma to his other side. That was a man in love if he'd ever seen one, a man happily and completely mired in his family. More and more often, Clay found himself wishing for what Garrett had with Emma.

It had been a long time coming, but at thirty-one, he was finally ready to settle down. And Veronica Evans, he told himself as he tucked the pretty blonde under his arm and smiled into her cool blue eyes, might finally be the woman he wanted to settle down with.

Involuntarily his gaze strayed back across the lawn to Maddie. Automatically his mind clicked into comparison mode. Veronica was exactly the kind of woman that Maddie, with her wild mop of dusky brown curls, her flashing black eyes, bohemian life-style, and razor-sharp tongue would never be. Veronica, he assured himself, ignoring an uncomfortable little niggle of dissent, was the kind of woman he'd been looking for all his life. She was drop-dead gorgeous, had impeccable taste and a sensible head on her shoulders. She was demure, solicitous and baked the hell out of every one of his favorite dishes. And she wasn't driven by her art the way Maddie was. She wasn't even particularly embroiled in her career. She was an officer in her daddy's bank and had made it clear as crystal that she could walk away from the position without a qualm if the incentive was right. She'd been subtle but not shy about clarifying that for Clay.

So what if she wasn't a brilliant conversationalist? Who cared if she wasn't overly imaginative and didn't seem to have many original thoughts? She was focused and centered, and what she was centered on was making him happy. Maddie Brannigan wouldn't know centered if it sneaked up and bit her on her saucy little tush.

The tush in question turned his way, presenting Clay with an unobstructed view of a tidy bottom packed into a pair of snug, bibbed, denim short shorts. The tiny flame-red T-shirt tucked under the bib hugged sweet, saucy breasts and left her midriff bare—just like the shorts bared tanned, toned legs that, as short as they were, were shapely and much more sexy than they ought to be.

"I don't know about you," Veronica said, the cool silk of her voice drawing his attention away from the trim little package of trouble and back where it belonged, "but I'm getting thirsty. Stay put. I'll get us some lemonade."

With a quick, adoring smile, she headed for the table loaded with refreshments, her pastel sundress swishing softly around her calves.

Clay braced to take a good-natured razzing when little brother Jesse sauntered up beside him.

"So it's lemonade, now, is it? My, oh, my. Last I knew, a cold beer was more your drink of choice. Amazing what a good woman can do for a sorry sinner."

Like all the James boys, Jesse's dark hair was thick and supple, even if it was a little longer and a little more recklessly styled than his own or Garrett's. The wide mouth that grinned at Clay mirrored his own—as did the electric blue of Jesse's eyes. Unlike his older brothers, however, Jesse's eyes were so full of mischief and mayhem, one look provoked mothers to hustle their daughters out of sight and lock them away until he blew back out of town.

Taking Jesse's ribbing in stride, Clay assumed the *wiser* brother role and clapped a hand on Jesse's shoulder. "You ought to think about finding a good woman yourself, little brother. One who'd knock some sense into that hard head of yours and make a respectable man out of you."

Jesse, the true renegade of the James clan, just grinned his outlaw grin and thumbed back his black Resistol.

"Respectable?" He affected a full-body shudder. "Bite your tongue. Garrett's respectable enough for the three of us. But something tells me," he added in a speculative aside, "you might be thinking about joining the ranks."

Clay's gaze tracked back to Maddie where she was the center of attention of a gaggle of chest-puffing, macho-posturing males. Disgusted, he sought Jesse's opinion of Veronica. "So what do you think of her?"

Jesse tipped back his long neck then scratched his jaw. "Guess that'd depend on how serious you are."

Maddie's laughter rang on the summer wind like the deep, mellow tones of a heavy brass wind chime, charming the testosterone in the air around her to a new high. It also coaxed back Clay's gaze just as she tossed her hair over her shoulder with a flirty lift of her chin.

An irritating little tick sent a muscle twitching above his left eye. Determined to ignore it and her, he tuned in to Jesse's cryptic comment. "Depends on how serious I am? What's that supposed to mean? Either you like Veronica or you don't."

"I like her fine," Jesse assured him quickly. "It's just…I don't know." He paused to measure Clay's reaction. "She seems a little tame for you is all. Besides, I always thought you had a thing for Maddie."

Clay whipped his head around. "Maddie?" He barked out a short laugh. "What under God's own Wyoming sky, would make you think I was interested in that irritating, infuriating, fire-breathing little shrew?" He threw in a snort for good measure. "If ever there was a woman who would *not* be on my list of marriage candidates, it would be her."

Jesse grinned. "It's your story, so you can tell it any way you want to. But if I was a betting man, I'd stake my gold buckles you've got a bad itch for that little filly."

Clay shook his head. "These rodeo analogies are real cute, Jess, and your women may fall for that cowboy quaint philosophy, but if you think I'm interested in Mad Dog Brannigan, you've been thrown one too many times and lit on your head just a little too often."

In truth, Jesse's record and current standings in the Pro Rodeo Cowboy Association indicated just the opposite. It took a real bad day and a killer bull to toss Jesse James into the dirt before an eight count these days.

But he was also more astute than his brother wanted to give him credit for. Jesse figured he had a bead on the reason Clay always watched Maddie and for the deep scowl darkening his face when he did. The look on Garrett's face when he strolled over to join them said he had Clay pegged, too.

"I don't know if the neighborhood can stand this much of the James brain trust huddled in one place," Garrett said with a grin. "Care to fill me in on what this little meeting of the minds is about?"

Jesse tipped his half-full beer bottle at Clay. "Our bull-headed brother here is trying to convince me he doesn't have the hots for Maddie."

Garrett snorted. "Oh, *that* same old saw."

"What is it with you two?" Clay grumbled, slicing a glare between them. "When did I ever give anyone the impression that Maddie Brannigan inspired anything but heartburn?"

Garrett and Jesse exchanged knowing looks.

"Okay," Clay grudgingly admitted, knowing he couldn't completely dodge their accusations. "So she's a hot little number. So maybe I have wondered—on an occasion or two, when I could have been declared temporarily but legally insane—what she'd be like in bed. But that's just curiosity. And I'm not stupid. Neither do I have a death wish. The woman is Looney Tunes. The woman is certifiable. Besides, she hates my guts.

"Forget about it," he insisted, determined not to rise any higher to the bait they were dangling when his brothers exchanged another look. "I know what I want in a woman. I know what I need. I need a woman who will be happy with home and hearth, taking care of me and making babies."

"Sounds logical," Garrett said with a condescending and totally insincere nod. "Not to mention self-serving."

"And boring," Jesse added, making it clear that he thought Clay was dirt stupid and up to his eyeballs in illusion if he thought Veronica would be enough of a challenge. "Kind of like settling for chicken soup when you could have hot chili."

"Just because you've got Emma," Clay grumbled, even though he was happy with Garrett's good fortune for finding someone who was not only all of the things he himself wanted in a mate but her own woman, too. "And you," he added with a clipped nod at Jesse, "just because you've made it your life's work to test drive as many models as is humanly possible before you settle on the one that's right for you, doesn't mean I'm in a position to do that, either.

"Nope," he insisted, building on his conviction and irked that it sounded like he was working harder to convince himself than his brothers. "I don't have your good fortune, Garrett, or your stamina, Jess. Maddie Brannigan? No way, no how, no chance."

Then he walked away to join Veronica, who had been waylaid by the minister who had renewed Garrett and Emma's vows at the church service earlier.

One of these days, maybe he'd have a little talk with

Pastor Considine himself, he thought, then scowled as the sight of a brilliant red T-shirt and way too much tanned, bare skin flitted by his peripheral vision and set his eye twitching again.

One

It wasn't even his birthday, and yet a big fat present had just been dropped in Clay's lap.

"Well would you look at that?" Sporting a huge grin, he slowed his tan Jeep Cherokee to a crawl and pulled over onto the shoulder of the highway.

Slinging his arm over the seat back, he angled a look behind him and backed up to the car stalled by the side of the road.

A beach-ball sun, apricot-gold and rimmed in shimmering silver was just crawling behind the Tetons, settling in for the night and taking the bulk of its warmth with it. Even though it was early August and the temperature had risen to the low eighties in the afternoon, a dusk chill was only a few minutes away. So was darkness. This stretch of blacktop was no place for friend or foe—or fowl, he added with a shake of his head and a chuckle—to be stalled.

He slid out of the Jeep and tugged his Stetson low over

his brow. Then, schooling a straight face, he tucked his fingers into the front pockets of his jeans and strolled leisurely over to the stranded car.

"Problem?" he asked, leaning an elbow on the roof of Maddie Brannigan's apple red compact and peering down into the open driver's-side window.

The big, yellow chicken behind the wheel clapped her beak together, crossed her wings over her breast, and let out a weary sigh. "It had to be you, didn't it?"

Giving in to the grin, he took a long, thorough survey of the woman trussed up in yellow feathers and a sour scowl. "Call it divine intervention," he said cheerfully and got ready to enjoy himself—*really* enjoy himself—at her expense.

She looked plump and ready to pluck in that get-up, but he knew exactly what the feathered finery covered—a sweet, sexy little body that he suspected was just short of smoldering with both anger and humiliation. He had every intention of pushing her to flash point. It was, after all, tradition.

From the time they were kids growing up as back-door neighbors on adjoining spreads, she'd made it her life's work to irritate him. Because she did such a good job of it, he'd returned the favor every chance he got and made it his personal mission to tick her off.

"On your way to a poultry convention?" he asked conversationally.

The heat in her eyes mirrored the sun's as she stared straight ahead, her glare fixed on the bumper of his Jeep as if she wished she had the horsepower to ram it into next Sunday.

"I know that riding-off-into-the-sunset scenes are reserved for hero types," she said, her words clipped and just this side of surly, "but just the same, why don't you try to stretch your limits...see if you can make it work for you."

He graced her with a shocked, and thoroughly staged, scowl. "What? You're suggesting I leave you here to fend for yourself? One lowly chicken against the elements? I wouldn't think of it."

She tried to lower her forehead to the steering wheel, but her beak got in the way. He cleared his throat to stall a chuckle and dipped his head in time to see her shoulders droop with her slow sigh of resignation.

"You're never going to let me hear the end of this, right?"

His grin spread wide. "And they say chickens have bird brains."

When she turned abruptly toward him, her beak cleared the open window and jabbed him in the nose.

He let out a surprised yelp and made a big show of checking for damage. "No need to get hostile. I'm here to help, so put that thing away."

"Oh, just stow it, James," she grumbled, then sent him scrambling when she shoved the door open.

Large orange chicken feet hit the pavement with twin slaps. A flurry of yellow feathers swirled above striped orange chicken legs as she flounced out of the car and started plodding down the highway.

Standing with his arms crossed over his chest, his weight slung on one leg, he enjoyed the sight for a moment before offering helpfully, "You know, if you flap a little harder, you might get some lift under those wings and save yourself a few steps."

"Ha-ha. Why don't you stand in the middle of the highway?" she suggested over her shoulder. "If you're lucky, the next vehicle by will be a semi. The impact will be quick and relatively painless and then we'll both be out of our misery."

Grinning openly now, Clay lazily sprinted the ten yards

it took to catch up with her. "I'd be happy to give you a lift."

She snorted. "I'd rather take my chances on becoming road kill."

He laughed out loud. "Isn't that a little like biting off your beak to spite your face?"

"Humph."

"Oh, come on," he wheedled, snagging her by a wing. "It's ten miles to town. It'll be dark soon, and then you'll be a prime target for some myopic duck hunter."

Though she dragged her three-toed feet, she finally let out a defeated sigh and grumpily let him steer her back to the Jeep.

"There," he said, patronizing and sympathetic to a fault when she settled with a disgruntled flurry on the passenger side. "Is this so bad?"

She stared straight ahead as he buried the clutch, shifted into low and eased back onto the pavement.

He knew he should probably feel guilty for getting such a bang out of needling her. He even considered backing off. A second was about as long as that malevolent thought lived, though, before it died a quick and unremarkable death. If the situation were reversed, he knew that Maddie Brannigan, with her blade-sharp tongue and snide little smiles would be enjoying herself every bit as much as he was—so he was going to milk this opportunity for all it was worth.

"Not one more word," she warned him, when he opened his mouth to make another crack. "I was on my way to a costume party, okay?"

"Whatever you say," he conceded, but with enough skepticism to earn another flouncy sputter.

A fuzzy yellow feather float by his nose. "What—now you're molting?"

Silence.

"So," he began again, relishing the prospect of ruffling a few more feathers, "you were going to a costume party..."

She eyed him with suspicion, then shrugged and filled in the blanks. "And the apple sputtered, stuttered and died."

"Maybe its allergic to—" he paused to flick at another piece of yellow fluff that drifted over to attach itself to the brim of his hat "—poultry."

Her smile was snide and long-suffering. "You're a Kentucky-fried bucket full of laughs, James. Just take me home and I'll call the garage to come and get my car." Then she muttered under her breath something to the tune of, "If the batteries hadn't died in my cell phone, I wouldn't have to put up with his lip or his twisted sense of humor."

"You want me to turn around and take you to the party?" he offered, as if the thought had just struck him. "Were they counting on you for...eggs or something?"

He swore he saw smoke wafting up from the top of her head as she slanted him a look that warned she would pluck his eyes out if he made one more crack.

Then she sat in martyred silence, refusing to give him so much as a glare while he whistled the jingle to a fast-food chicken chain the rest of the way into Jackson.

Two weeks later, Maddie Brannigan perched on the edge of the chair behind her overflowing desk in her tiny office at Necessities, and tried to ignore a month's worth of book work. She hated the business aspect of Necessities but loved everything else about the gallery she'd opened seven years ago to showcase her own original pieces of pottery and to promote multiple-media work by local artisans.

The gallery was thriving today. She could proudly and without reservation claim that it had been her own sweat and determination, a natural eye for art, and what people described as a knack for salesmanship that had made Necessities so successful.

Luck, she freely admitted, had played a part in it, too. But she figured a little luck enhanced most success stories and anyone who disputed that factor was either a fool or an egomaniac.

Maddie considered herself neither. She saw herself as pragmatic and sensible, even though she had taken a chance on Necessities in a highly competitive community of prolific artists.

Some people would argue—Clay James came instantly to mind—that she was eccentric. Some people—again Clay's pressed Wranglers, supple leather vests and impeccable tan Stetson flashed in her mind's eye—would label her as bohemian, maybe even flamboyant. She really didn't care what some people—Clay in particular—thought of her.

So what if she liked her skirts long and loose and flowing and preferred dangly, colorful earrings to neat little studs. It was nobody's concern but her own if she'd rather go barefoot than wear shoes, and had given up on taming her springy shoulder-length curls with little more than the occasional help from a brightly colored scarf.

None of those choices meant she was quirky. She simply liked color and flash, a little razzle with her dazzle. The way she dressed, the way she approached life, with eyes wide open but ready to embrace any adventure, was merely a reflection of, maybe even an extension of, her love for her art. "Necessities" had been born and nurtured by that love.

She could have taken another road. Her SAT scores had soared off the charts; the academic scholarships offered by many prestigious universities had been numerous and humbling. The eternal disappointment that her parents had little success concealing when she'd chosen her potter's wheel, glazes and kiln over a more lucrative and respectable career in law or medicine had been difficult to ignore.

The major incentive behind her hard work had been her desire to prove to them that she didn't need to become a doctor like her sister or a lawyer like her brother to be a success. That and the occasional bothersome need to eat.

Thinking of her family now made her realize how much she missed them. Since their retirement, her parents spent little time on their Jackson Hole ranch where they'd raised Maddie, Savannah and Ryan. Instead, they spent more and more time at their Palm Springs condo. Following their lead, Savannah and Ry had migrated to the flash and frenzy of the West Coast several years ago. Maddie rarely saw any of them. She regretted that. Really regretted it.

Tonight, she promised herself, tonight she'd give them all a call—even though she knew her mother wouldn't waste much time before asking her if she was any closer to settling down and giving her grandchildren like her sister had.

Only on that count did she feel inferior to her younger sibling. *Inferior* probably wasn't the word she was searching for, but it was the one that came to mind, anyway. Savannah was already a parent. Ry was engaged, so a family was inevitable for him, too. And while Maddie didn't envy either of them their high-profile careers, she did envy Savannah her babies.

Refusing to let herself get melancholy over the lack of someone special in her life, or the more pronounced absence of a child of her own to nurture and cherish, she forced herself to get on to the business at hand.

Fiancés, husbands, babies or even Necessities, wasn't foremost on her mind today. Neither was the world's perception of her personal style. Something else entirely occupied her thoughts as she drew a deep breath, picked up the phone and punched in a number.

While she waited, the simmering sort of anticipation that she always felt when facing the prospect of going toe-to-toe with Clay James sizzled through her blood. When his secretary, Agnes Crawford, answered on the third ring and announced that she'd reached the James Construction Company, Maddie settled herself down.

After giving Agnes a cheerful hello and inquiring about her health and her grandchildren, she asked to be connected with Clay. Then, leaning back in her chair, she propped her feet on the corner of her desk, crossed her ankles and waited.

Only a few moments passed before a deceptively charming and sinfully sexy male voice came on the line. "Hello, this is Clay. What can I do for you?"

A spike of irritation and an unsolicited shiver of awareness shimmied up her spine.

"Clay," she said, inflicting just enough greeting in her tone to sound cordial. "It's Maddie."

A short silence was followed by, "Well, hey, Chicken Little. How's it flappin'?"

She didn't need to see his face to know he was grinning like a loon. Resisting the urge to suggest that he take his worn-out chicken jokes and stuff them where the sun don't shine, she ground her teeth, drew a deep breath and forged ahead. "I was wondering if you've set a construction date yet."

"Construction date," he repeated to the sound of shuffling paper. "You know what? I think maybe we have. Hold on a sec. I'll dig up the schedule."

As she waited, she thought back to the decision she'd made to enlist Clay and Garrett to build her new gallery. The first reason was room. The present location—a rented building squashed between a music shop and a trading post—was no longer large enough to accommodate her inventory. The second was practicality.

While Garrett's wife, Emma, was Maddie's dearest friend, friendship hadn't come into play in her decision. The bottom line here was that despite a long, haranguing history with Clay that had started when they were kids and never played itself out, she really did have a head for business. Clay and Garrett's construction company was the best-run outfit and the best value around. And although she'd had to swallow some pride—not a new occurrence around Clay—she'd looked past their long-standing rivalry, fallen in love with the blueprints he'd drawn up and sealed a deal.

Checking on the construction date, however, wasn't the real reason she was calling Clay today. It was a smoke screen. She had another, more compelling, issue—revenge—and the sweet, thrilling certainty that it was within her grasp.

If asked, she wouldn't have been able to explain this constant competition the two of them had going. Neither would Clay. It was an element in their lives that neither gave conscious thought. Like dogs hassled cats, like Hatfields feuded with McCoys, the rivalry, the incessant knee-jerk need to constantly dish out grief, had just always been there. It had been there so long, in fact, neither of them bothered to ask themselves why they persisted or what they were gaining in the process.

In fact, it had evolved so far that to ask why they were always going at each other would be like asking why the sky was blue or why the mountains where high. The why of it didn't matter. It was just the way it was.

Maybe it had started when they were toddlers using their chubby little baby fists to steal each other's teething rings. Could be it was in elementary school when they'd gone head-to-head in spelling bees or on the playground at recess playing tag. By junior high, when they'd vied for everything from delegate seats on the student council to class officers, it was out of control.

Whatever the reason, however petty the original cause, Maddie gave it as much thought today as she ever did—none—as she waited for Clay to come back on the line.

It had been two weeks since the chicken suit incident. Even though his appearance on the scene had been by accident not design, it was another event in a long string where he'd gotten his chuckles at her expense. Now it was payback time—maybe a little slow in coming—but all the sweeter for her wait.

"Still there?" he asked as he picked up the phone again.

"I'm here," she said evenly, and told herself the ripple of awareness that lapped through her body was not sexual, but the prospect of retaliation.

Admittedly his voice—brandy rich and bourbon mellow—held a sensual promise that reduced most women to ridiculous little sighs and simpery palpitations. She, however, was not most women. The only reaction she felt, she assured herself, was the irritating knowledge that he knew what kind of effect he had on the opposite sex.

"What did you come up with?" she asked, when she realized she'd been dwelling on the sound of his voice and arguing with herself about its effect on her for too long.

"Well…" More paper crackled in the background. She could picture him wedging the receiver between his ear and a broad shoulder. "Ah, here we go. You'll like this. It looks like you're next on the list. Garrett's got the permits and the crew lined up. Most of the material came in last week, so if nothing comes up in the meantime to slow us down, figure on next Monday to break ground. That work for you?"

"That works just fine." Despite herself, she couldn't contain her excitement over the prospect of seeing her gallery take shape after months in the planning stages.

"Do I have to remind you that if you've got any alterations you want made on the blueprints," he added, "now's the time to tell us."

"No. No, I think we got everything ironed out."

"Now see, it's that kind of statement that'll get us in trouble. *Thinking* everything is ironed out isn't good enough, Matilda. You've got to *know* you're solid on the plans because once we get started, there won't be any room for changes."

As usual, both his superior male attitude and his implication that if there were problems on the horizon she'd be the one to cause them, set the fillings in her teeth tingling. Just as predictably, his ingratiating habit of calling her by her given name conjured visions of voodoo dolls and pins. Lots of pins. Lots of sharp pins.

"I get the point," she enunciated testily. "I *know* everything's pinned down. Okay? There won't be any changes."

"Good. Then we're understood. And we ought to ease through this just fine."

It was more threat than promise. More wish than expectation. They both knew the chances of the two of them *easing* through the building project were roughly the same as a 747 *easing* through the eye of a needle.

A silence filled with all kinds of bloody scenarios passed before he said, "Well then, now that we've got that straight, was there anything else?"

The hint of dismissal in his tone rankled. But then, everything about him irritated her—always had. Clay James was too confident, too competitive and too damn pretty. All the James boys were. With Clay, however, we were talking overkill. His thick black hair, light blue eyes and cowboy lean build completed a package that was too poster-perfect for his or anyone else's good.

And there had always been something else about Clay and his button-down neatness and organized orderly life.

Something that grated and gnawed and, as much as she hated to admit it, intrigued her. She was darned if today was the day she would let herself think about why. He was, after all, a man who had made it his life's work to be a major thorn in her side.

That's why it was so disturbing that if she was brutally honest, she'd have to admit how sometimes—emphasis on *sometimes*—she found herself enjoying their verbal skirmishes. Worse, she sometimes wondered what it would be like to be on his good side.

It shouldn't, but it miffed her that he reserved his orneriness for her and his excess charm for everyone else. For her he'd perfected a teasing brand of arrogance that hit all her hot spots and set her blood boiling with the need for retaliation.

He'd done it again just now. He'd pushed her hot button by wanting to get rid of her.

"What's the matter, Clayton," she purred nastily, the needling coming as naturally as blinking. "Are you pressed for time today? Could it be the banking Betty Crocker is waiting in the wings with a little offer of cash and casserole?"

He answered her accusation with a short silence, then a silken taunt. "Why, if I didn't know better, I'd think I'd just heard a little green in your voice, Miss Brannigan," he went on with irritating smugness, "I'm flattered—baffled, but flattered—that you're jealous of Veronica."

"In your dreams, home boy," she muttered, shrugging off that little absurdity with a laugh then ruined the effect by backpedaling. "I just find it a little distasteful that you'd let pleasure interfere with business. After all, I'm going to be throwing a lot of money your way. The least you could do is make time to talk with me."

"Don't you worry, sweet cheeks." Though he shot for placating, the undertone of PO'd male came through loud and clear. It made her smile. Anytime she could get to Clay James, she was a happy girl.

"We'll earn every penny and you know it," he went on as she grinned into the receiver. "But, if you want to talk business, then hey, talk away."

Actually, she'd finished talking business. And thanks to her smart mouth and her unfailing need to be a squeak in his hinges, she'd just about tripped herself up. With two well-directed hits, he'd managed to put her somewhere in the vicinity of "hung by her own rope."

"My mistake," she countered, recovering quickly by eating more crow than she had the stomach for, "for even thinking you'd shirk business for pleasure."

Another measuring silence followed.

"Well," he said finally, "*was* there something else?"

"Actually..." Regrouping, she picked her words carefully. This, after all, was the real reason she'd called. This was the setup. This was the payoff. "There is something I wanted to talk to you about. You may have heard...I'm the chair for the variety show this year. Sounds like I'll be directing it, too."

Jackson Hole, for all its integrated mix of migrated multimillionaires and home-grown locals, was full of community spirit. The annual variety show, organized by the Chamber of Commerce and staged with the help of volunteers, was a substantial source of revenue for the hospital. The proceeds from this year's show were earmarked for the children's wing.

"And," he prompted, making her ask the question they both knew he would say yes to.

"And I've been designated to ask if you would be willing to do a segment again this year."

His deep breath sighed across the line. "Don't you think the singing cowboy bit is wearing a little thin?"

It was true. Clay, with his cowboy lean looks, his more-than-modest ability to coax sweet chords from his twelve-string Gibson, and a voice, which, if he'd gone in that direction, may have ended up on the country charts, was a regular, repeat feature in the annual event. But every year the committee had requests to hear him again, so every year they asked. And every year, prompted by his own sense of community spirit—and, Maddie suspected snidely, his ego—he agreed. It was his ego she was counting on to set the trap.

"Actually, I was thinking of something a little different this year," she said, working to conceal the plotting in her voice. "Are you up for it?"

He sighed heavily. "Yeah, sure. Why not. Just don't put me in a dress, and I'm your man."

She mouthed a silent "Yes!" and punched a triumphant fist in the air. "That's great, Clay. I thank you. The hospital thanks you. I'll get back to you a little closer to the rehearsal dates," she added demurely. "In the meantime, mark your calendar for the Labor Day weekend and we'll count on you."

Before he could pick up on her smug sense of satisfaction, she disconnected, sprang out of her chair and did a jaunty little victory lap around her office.

Two

She didn't put him in a dress. Well, *technically*, it wasn't a dress. Technically, it was more of a banana yellow bolero skirt with a rainbow of trailing ruffles. The size-twelve heels matched perfectly.

"No way," Clay snarled, getting right in Maddie's face as he clutched the skirt and middy top in one big masculine fist and the pineapple and mixed-fruit headdress and a pair of yellow hoop earrings in the other. "If you think I'm going to parade around on stage like a drag queen doing Carmen Miranda, you're out of your ever-loving mind."

The rest of the cast milled quietly around on the fringes of the action, sneaking covert looks at their director, Maddie Brannigan, and the designated, but balking star of the "Chiquita Banana" skit, Clay James. Even if someone wanted to intervene to ward off the possibility of physical blows, they were enjoying the verbal sparring far too much to interrupt it.

Maddie was doing some enjoying of her own. She was enjoying the heck out of Clay's red-faced anger. She was particularly pleased by the way the veins in his neck had popped out like tire treads. And she loved like blue blazes that she was the one who had set him off.

She didn't let herself dwell on it, but the reality was that, chest-puffing mad and nostril-flaring agitated, he was one magnificent male animal. Steady as a post, telling herself she was above reacting to him on a physical level, she faced him down, warming to the thrill of the battle that she knew was hers to win.

"But you said you'd be glad to do something different this year," she reasoned, all innocence and astonishment.

"Different, not deviant," he growled, shaking the fist that held the crumpled wad of ruffles and sequins. "I'm not wearing this."

"It's not deviant. It's funny. And it's a little late to back out now, Clay. You'll let the whole cast down."

"Oh, no you don't." He slowly shook his head, tried for an in-control sneer. "You're not going to shame me into this. And you can bat those baleful brown eyes until the cows come home. That melting-chocolate look you've got perfected might work on your little legion of admirers, but it's not going to work on me."

Once more with feeling she blinked, big and huge and innocent, absurdly pleased that he thought she had a legion—even a small one—of admirers.

He swore under his breath. "You could have told me," he ground out between teeth clenched so tight the muscles in his jaw bulged.

"You could have come to rehearsal," she countered and knew she had him there, "then this close to show time, it wouldn't have come as such a surprise. But you were too busy."

"Too busy framing up your gallery," he growled, so

close to her face she could smell the cool hint of mint on his breath that was so at odds with the heat of his temper. "Dammit, Maddie. You think you've pulled one over on me, but you've singed your own feathers this time, because I'm not doing this bit."

"Well," she said, with a staged sigh of concession, "if that's the way you feel. But I've got to tell you, I never dreamed you'd be so uncomfortable or uncertain of your masculinity that you'd be intimidated by a little good-natured fun."

His glare was so hot she felt skewered, basted and barbecued. Lord he was mad. She loved it. And the way that little muscle above his eye twitched—a sure sign he was about ready to blow—almost had her laughing out loud with glee. Almost.

She used a deep breath to get ahold of herself. "Well, I guess we'll just have to scratch the skit then." Her shoulders rose and fell with another heavy sigh. "It's a shame, though. The Methodist church auxiliary went to such trouble making the costumes. And along with the skits on the other old commercials from the baby-boomer era, the 'Chiquita Banana' piece was the pivotal number for the segment."

"You can get someone else to do it," he muttered testily, but with just enough guilt in his tone that she knew she was wearing him down.

"At this late date? I don't think so. Besides, word's already spread that you're in the show again this year, but that you're doing something out of the ordinary."

Emma James, pianist for this year's production, sat in the orchestra pit watching the verbal combat going on, on center stage. Clay's brother Garrett, who had just stopped by to see how much longer it would be before rehearsal would be over and Emma would be coming home, dropped onto the piano bench beside her. Together they watched the show within a show.

"She's playing him like a spinet," Emma said with an amused shake of her head.

"Set him up like a pro," Garrett agreed, thoroughly enjoying seeing his cooler-than-cool brother being taken to task by a master. "Do you suppose they'll ever figure out that they're crazy about each other?"

"Maybe," Emma said thoughtfully. "Let's just hope it happens before there's bloodshed."

In the relative obscurity of the pit, Garrett pulled his wife close to his side and kissed her sweetly. "Got to run. Take notes, okay? I want to hear every detail when you get home."

As Garrett slipped quietly out of the theater, the action on stage intensified.

Maddie was just getting warmed up. She still had her trump card to play. "Well, Clay, if that's really the way you feel about it..." Weary with disappointment, she looked toward the backstage curtain. "Sara—are you back there, sweetie?"

Emma and Garrett's daughter, eight-year-old Sara Jane, was Clay's one-and-only niece. Since Maddie and Emma were best friends, Sara looked toward Maddie as family, too. And Maddie loved her like she was her own. When Sara had begged to help with the variety show, Maddie had made sure she'd found some task for the little girl to perform.

"Sara, honey," Maddie said when Sara Jane skipped out onto the stage. "Can you take your uncle Clay's costume back to Mrs. Claypool and tell her we won't be able to use it? He's decided not to be in the show this year."

Sara stared from her uncle Clay, who she adored, to her "aunt" Maddie and back to Clay again. Her big brown eyes brimmed with disappointment. "You're not gonna be in the show? But, Uncle Clay, you're *always* in the show."

Clay narrowed his eyes at Maddie. She gave him a "you explain it to her" look before he shifted his attention back to Sara Jane.

One look at her crestfallen expression and Maddie knew his heart had turned to mush. And when Sara innocently asked, "What if we don't raise enough money for the children's wing to get their computer 'cause people find out you're not in the show?" evidently, his mind turned to mush, too, because the next words out of his mouth were, "Don't you worry, sweet pea. I'll do it."

Sara Jane wrapped her arms around him in a flash as he bent to scoop her up and hug her hard against his chest.

Maddie grinned, smug and victorious, as Clay mouthed a silent, "You'll pay for this," over the top of Sara's head.

Maddie only smiled and, with the authority of a Steven Spielberg, clapped her hands together to get the cast's attention. "Okay, people," she said then snapped out her orders. "Let's get in our places and take it from the top."

He stole the show. In his fruit-laden turban, with his broad hairy chest busting out above the knotted middy top and his size twelves teetering on banana yellow heels, Clay James brought the house down.

He *was* the "Chiquita Banana" girl. And no woman, man or child could ever mistake the hip-swinging samba or the hairy, muscular legs that peeked out between the trailing ruffles of his slit skirt for anything but six feet two inches of one-hundred-percent American male singing and cha-chaing across the stage and having some fun at his own expense for a good cause.

At the cast party afterward, Maddie couldn't even be miffed that as he usually managed to do, he'd turned the tables on her again. What had started out as a plot to sully his ego had evolved into a romp of a performance that had been so much fun, even she felt compelled to congratulate him.

"Well, Clayton," she said, marching up to where he stood with some of the other cast members rehashing the show, "I've got to tell you—you outdid yourself with that one."

Before he could do more than flash a cocky grin in acknowledgment of her compliment, Veronica, sophisticated and demurely sexy in a slim, black slip dress, wedged her way gracefully along Clay's side. She pressed a glass of champagne into his hand. "A little bubbly for the top banana," she cooed with a possessive smile.

Baffled by the urge to mess up Veronica's artfully styled hair and clip her perfectly manicured nails down to the quick, Maddie let herself be wedged away from his growing circle of well-wishers. For some unknown reason, she resented the heck out of Veronica's intrusion. She'd wanted to share the show's success with Clay. They'd both worked hard on it—as had all the volunteers. Veronica's presence after the fact at the party—even though cast members were free to invite their spouses or significant others, and even though Veronica had supplied most of the party snacks—felt like an unwelcome intrusion.

Her resentment, she decided, really had nothing to do Veronica. Veronica was okay. And it had absolutely nothing to do with wishing she was in Veronica's shoes. Frankly, she mused, ashamed of the nasty little thought that developed, she wouldn't be caught at her own funeral in those shoes, literally or figuratively. Ugly, skimpy, spiky things. She shuddered and wiggled her toes in her comfy sandals that peeked out beneath the flowing folds of her gauzy print skirt.

On a less-literal note, she was not and had never been interested in Clay James on a personal level. No, she assured herself. It wasn't personal. It would never be personal. A romantic involvement would be ludicrous. Laughable. Which made her huffy little pique all the more puzzling.

The problem, she decided as she stood there, slowly nursing her champagne and covertly studying his profile—realizing as she did that she'd never noticed that sexy little bump on the bridge of his nose that somehow managed to enhance the perfection instead of mar it—

But I digress, she mused irritably and cut off that unprecedented little side trip by picking up on her original train of thought: the problem was that seeing Clay with Veronica bothered her because she thought Clay could do better than the socially adept bake-off queen. The problem, she continued, warming to her logic, had nothing to do with the niggling notion that if Clay James really wanted a woman, that she, herself, would make an exceedingly better match for him.

Not that she wanted to be, she assured herself quickly. And definitely not that she cared. She didn't. Not even a little bit. He was too neat and tidy and way too regimented for her. And way, way too bossy.

Tapping a finger thoughtfully to her upper lip, she drifted toward the table of hors d'oeuvres as Veronica's carefully modulated laughter drifted across the room.

At the sound Maddie gave the mental equivalent of a snort. Veronica only thought she knew how to handle Clay. In actuality, the svelte blond beauty didn't have a clue. And while Maddie really had nothing against her personally, she knew Veronica wouldn't be enough woman for Clay.

That man needed someone with a little fire. A little zip. A little something that would keep him on his toes and wanting to come home at night for something less benign than a home-cooked meal and a shoulder massage.

She tipped her champagne to her lips, thinking that *she'd*

know how to handle him. Thinking that she *could* handle him if she wanted to.

But you don't want to, she reminded herself staunchly. Just like you don't want to know what it would be like to kiss him.

She diverted her attention to the food table, popped a shrimp puff into her mouth—most likely one of Veronica's—and refused to acknowledge that it was delicious. What she couldn't refuse, however, was dealing with why she was thinking about kissing Clay.

She'd had the chance to kiss him once, and not that long ago. She'd been so royally ticked off at him at the time, though, that if he'd come anywhere near her with his mouth, she'd have cheerfully bitten off his tongue. If she remembered right, she'd even threatened him with the probability.

With a rueful smile, she continued drifting around the fringes of the party, deliberately separating herself from the clusters of animated conversations and post-production anecdotes. Before she'd realized what she was doing, her gaze had sought Clay again where he stood across the room with his arm slung casually over Veronica's shoulders. Veronica, of course, always busy scoring points, ogled him with her best puppy dog adoration.

She popped another shrimp puff, promised herself she would *not* ask Veronica for the recipe, and found her thoughts wandering back to the night she'd been kissing-close and physically compromised by Clay James at his outlaw best.

That's when it hit her. In a riveting moment of clarity, she realized that it had been that particular night and its volatile circumstances that was responsible for this unwanted and unsolicited awareness of Clay as a man.

Snagging a fresh glass of champagne from a nearby tray, she let herself remember. *Made* herself remember, as an exercise, she assured herself, in exorcising the demon known as Clayton Franklyn James.

This all went back to the night Garrett had kidnapped Emma...

They'd been separated for three months. Three painful, troubling months not only for the two of them but for their family and friends. Maddie had suffered with Emma when she'd suspected Garrett was having an affair. She'd taken Emma and Sara into her home—Emma broken, Sara confused—and tried to give her some thinking room. Just as painful as seeing Emma suffer, however, was the breach in the trust and friendship Maddie had always felt with Garrett.

Her first loyalty, though, had been with Emma. Because of that loyalty, she'd honored Emma's wishes and refused to let Garrett see her. When Clay had come to Maddie's door one midnight on the pretense of showing her the blueprints for her gallery, she should have known it was setup, but her eagerness to get her hands on the plans had made her an easy mark. While Clay kept her busy in the kitchen poring over the plans, Garrett had slipped into the apartment and stolen into a sleeping Emma's bedroom. When Maddie had finally figured out what was going on and threatened to call the police, Garrett was already on his way out the door with Emma in his arms—and Clay was taking the decoy role to new limits.

She'd dived for the phone to call the law; Clay had jerked the wire out of the jack. She'd lunged for the door; he'd tackled her. Amid a flurry of muffled curses, a tangle of limbs and the rustle of her silk nightgown, she'd ended up beneath Clay on the floor.

He'd been smug, and superior, and teasing in his easy command of her body as he'd pinned her hands above her head. She'd been furious. Bested again by the man who

had beaten her all her life in everything from swimming to
tennis to pool.

As angry as she'd been the night of the kidnapping,
though, something had happened as she'd lain beneath him.
Something she hadn't expected. She'd realized, with no
small amount of horror, that he'd gotten to her in a way
that was far different and much more disturbing than ever
before. He'd—

Someone brushed by her, jarring her out of her disturbing
reflections and back to the party. She smiled quickly, murmured, "It's okay," as Bob Thomas, one of the prop men,
apologized for jostling her before he moved off into the
crowd.

It took a few minutes, however, to calm the rapid-fire
beat of her heart and cool the flush that had heated her
cheeks.

Clay James had gotten to her that night, all right. He'd
gotten to her on an elemental level—a male-female level
that she'd been denying by ignoring ever since.

Well, she wasn't ignoring it now. As a matter of fact, as
she stood in the midst of this crowd of partying people,
suddenly she couldn't think about anything else.

That night…he'd felt so…so alive, so vital, so aggres-
sively, wonderfully male. Three entire months later she was
still critically aware of just *how* male as he'd lain above
her, the strength and the heat of his long, sinewy body
seeping into hers, the warm caress of his breath feathering
across her brow.

And he'd known, damn him. He'd known he was af-
fecting her, and he'd taunted her with the knowledge. The
subtle shift of his hips against hers, the intimate press of
his chest against her breasts. He'd stolen her breath, heated
her blood and set off a physical reaction that exceeded any
anger she'd ever felt toward him.

Even now, looking at him across a public room, she got

caught up remembering the lush stirrings he'd provoked—deep and warm and low. Even now, she got lost in the memory of the scent of him, the heat of him, and of how close they had come that night to crossing a line that may have changed things between them forever.

"I'd ask what's got you so deep in thought—" Clay's brother Garrett's voice snapped her head up and around as he joined her "—but something tells me it's none of my business. *Really* none of my business."

He extended a full glass of champagne and relieved her of her empty. Although she'd already passed her self-imposed limit of one glass, she accepted another with a trembling hand.

She'd been blessed with an olive complexion. Yet as she stood there, the object of Garrett's curious stare, she knew her summer tan was doing a poor job of concealing the pink that had crept into her cheeks.

She tipped back her glass before replying. "Actually," she said, then cleared her throat of the little Kermit that had crept in, "I was doing a little daydreaming."

"That much, I'd figured out," he teased with that trademark James grin that had melted hearts from Jackson to Cheyenne.

"Leave it to a man to put a sexual spin on an innocent fantasy." Though it was a little weak, she managed a smile to take the bite out of her reply.

"There *are* no innocent fantasies." He waggled a dark brow. "Only fun ones."

An honest grin tipped up the corners of her mouth this time. "Shame on you. You're a married man—and a father to boot."

"Happily married to the woman who fulfills all my fantasies," he clarified, as his gaze trailed the room until he found Emma. The blue of his eyes warmed like a summer sky when his wife met and returned his smile. The look

Garrett sent Emma was so full of secret intimacies it made Maddie feel like she was intruding on a private conversation.

With a wistful sigh, she wondered what it would feel like to be looked at that way. To be loved that way.

Although she'd been ready to hang Garrett out to dry a few months ago when she'd thought, along with Emma, that he'd been cheating, nothing pleased Maddie more than seeing them together again, and this happy.

On impulse, she rose to her toes and hugged him.

"And that would be for?" he asked, surprised by her show of affection but returning her sisterly embrace.

"That would be for being such a nice person."

A wealth of understanding passed between them with one brief, speaking look.

He gave her a quick squeeze then let her go with a gruff, "Ditto," that successfully brought to a close a scene that promised some sloppy sentiment they both acknowledged but didn't want to share in public.

"So," she said brightly and moved on to a safe, unemotional topic. "How'd you like the show?"

"Well, it's not quite ready for Broadway, but I'd pay to see it again—especially the banana boy."

She returned his grin. "He was something, wasn't he?"

"Oh, yeah. And there's not a *real* man in town who's likely to ever let him forget it."

They shared another quick smile.

"So what do you think of Clay and Veronica?"

Garrett's direct question caught her off guard. After a slight stumble, she squared her shoulders and got busy looking uninterested. "Actually, I hadn't thought about it," she lied, straight-facedly. "But now that you mention it, they do look pretty good together. Is it serious, do you think?"

Hoping to project casual interest, not the chest-tightening

apprehension she really didn't want to feel, she sipped more champagne.

Garrett studied her in a measuring silence, then shrugged. "I don't know. Maybe. I know he's got an itch to settle down."

"How convenient. Veronica looks like she knows just where to scratch."

When Garrett snorted out a quick laugh, then eyed her with a speculative grin, she busied herself ducking her chin and feigning fascination with the bubbles in her champagne.

"Tell me something, Maddie."

She looked up and then quickly away from a pair of eyes as blue as Clay's and far too probing. "What do you want to know?"

"Why is it that you and Clay have never done the dating thing?"

She barked out a laugh that was supposed to express incredulity. When she choked on it, though, it sort of diminished the effect. She was red-faced again, but this time from lack of oxygen when Garrett finally eased up pounding her on the back.

"Must have had a bone in it," she wheezed, pressing a hand to her throat.

"The champagne, or the idea of a romantic involvement with my brother?" he persisted.

When she didn't reply, couldn't reply, he pressed on. "Why don't you just admit that you've got a thing for him?"

"Oh, I've got a thing for him, all right," she conceded with a bobbing nod and a sarcastic and indelicate little grunt. "It's a thing like an allergy. It's irritating and it's persistent, but I've just got to live with the grief it dishes out."

"Have you ever considered," he said, refusing to let her

divert him, "that the reason he gives you such a hard time is because he's trying to get your attention?"

"He's gotten my attention. Several times," she acknowledged, thinking of all the times he'd embarrassed or beaten her. "And each time, he's made it very clear why he does it. He just loves to tick me off. I figure it's a man thing. Or a little boy thing—sort of a carryover from adolescence that he never outgrew."

"And why is that do you think?"

Darn the man. He was like a dog worrying a bone. She didn't want to think about why. Just like she didn't want to explore the possibilities Garrett was hinting at. No sir. The notion that Clay James might be attracted to her, arriving on the heels of her own latent but disturbing discovery that she was attracted to him, was just too unsettling to entertain.

"Why *can't* he let go of the tugging-pigtails-and-putting-frogs-in-my-lunch-bucket syndrome?" she asked, dodging his question with her Freudian tongue in her cheek. "My guess would be immaturity. Maybe a latent case of breast envy.

"No, seriously, think about it," she insisted with a devilish grin and a mental sigh of relief when Garrett's chuckle relayed that he'd given up on getting a straight answer. "Don't you think he was just a lit-tle too convincing in those heels tonight? And I wasn't going to say anything, but I noticed he hasn't turned them or the earrings back into wardrobe yet," she added in a confidential aside that broke Garrett up completely.

They were both laughing at the absolute impossibility of superstraight, supermacho Clay James with cross-dressing tendencies, when Clay sidled up beside them, sans Veronica, who Maddie concluded must have been surgically removed from his armpit.

"Care to let me in on your little joke?" he asked with a curious smile.

"No!" they both burst out in unison then dissolved into another fit of laughter at Clay's unwitting expense.

Garrett pinched the tears from his eyes, then shot Maddie a conspiratorial grin. "It's time for me to make a graceless exit. I'm going to find my wife, convince her it's time to go home to bed, then do a little research on that topic we were discussing earlier. And you might give a little thought to what we were talking about, too."

After a meaningful look, he slapped a hand to his brother's back. "See ya around, Banana Boy."

Then he headed across the room, leaving Maddie with a fading grin and Clay with a scowl as he tried to figure out what they'd been talking about.

A few awkward moments of silence passed before Maddie, prompted against her will to consider Garrett's suggestion, gave in to the urge and gave Clay an experimental smile. He looked so thunderstruck that she shook her head and raised her hand to touch his cheek.

It was pure knee-jerk reaction that had him snagging her wrist defensively and stalling it midair.

"Relax, James," she said with a tolerant grin. "I was just going to relieve you of a little rouge. Without the lipstick, it just doesn't work."

Eyes narrowed in distrust, he slowly unclasped his grip, then watched her face while she touched her fingers to his cheek to finish the job she'd started.

She was smiling softly when she swiped her fingers clean of the leftover makeup on the first handy napkin.

Clay was still scowling—and having a hard time figuring out why.

Had to be her smile, he reasoned. The woman was damn cute when she smiled. Cute, hell. She was sexy as sin, he decided as he weighed the unexpected wattage of a response that was foreign to him, unlike most of the single male population of Jackson Hole who knew the charm of Maddie Brannigan's smile all too well.

That nettled. Really nettled, he realized. She always had a smile for everyone but him. For him, she reserved her acid wit and watchdog snarl.

Until now. And now it actually seemed that *he* was the recipient of that sizzling, sexy grin for a change. As a matter of fact, if the notion hadn't been so ridiculous, he'd think she was diving way beyond the deep waters of tradition and was flirting with him.

He eyed her skeptically. Damn. She *was* flirting—and Maddie Brannigan was a horrible flirt. Well, actually, she wasn't horrible at all. She was actually pretty good at it. He'd just never expected to be on the receiving end of her multifaceted charms.

Suspicious but intrigued, he narrowed his brows, angled his chin and studied her face. It was, he admitted, a remarkable face. Rich with strength and self-assurance. Rare with an elegance that defied the untamed, gypsy-wild hair that framed it.

Too quickly his body reacted to the lush curve of her lower lip, the feathery little pulse beat fluttering at the hollow of her throat. Too exactly his mind played back to the feel of her wrist beneath his fingers, the touch of her fingertips on his cheek. Her fine bones were delicately structured, her silken skin, warm to the touch, as vital and compelling as the invitation in her melting brown eyes.

Then all too graphically his memory fired, triggering both tactile and vivid reminders of a night, three months past, when he'd wrestled her to the floor and pinned her there with his weight.

They'd been so close he'd been able to see each individual, spiky eyelash, smell the exotic, spicy fragrance of her shampoo, and feel, without a doubt, that she no longer needed help filling out her bra like she had when she was fourteen.

When he'd held himself above her, pressed himself against her, he'd had to draw on every Boy Scout gene in his body to keep from taking her—there. Right there on the floor. The way he'd never dreamed of taking her before.

He'd wanted to. Lord, knew he'd wanted to. And in her eyes he'd seen she wanted it too.

Now, months later, as he stood here trying to get a bead on what her smile was all about, he realized the wanting had never gone away. Not on his part. Evidently, not on hers, either.

Only a fool would take her up on the invitation she offered with her eyes. In fact, it took everything in *this* fool not to drag her tight against him, lose himself in those liquid depths and devour the lush warmth her wanton little mouth promised.

That mouth. He couldn't take his eyes off it. Couldn't stop himself from leaning toward her. He was lost in contemplating the delicious heat and woman softness of her body, when someone jostled him from behind and forced him to stumble over his better judgment.

With a quick snap of his head he took a mental step backward—then a physical one. He slogged in a deep breath. Let it out. Raked a shaking hand through his hair.

This was all too weird. This was all too strange. Maddie Brannigan hated his guts. And he had a solid dislike for hers. Besides, he had what he wanted in a woman—he had...he had...what the hell was her name?

Veronica! Of course. He had Veronica. He wanted Veronica.

Panicked because he'd just left her, and not only had her name momentarily escaped him but he couldn't get a clear picture of her face in his mind, he did the one thing that felt right. The one thing that felt safe. The one thing that felt sane. He decided to make Mad Dog growl.

"Why, my dear Ms. B.," he drawled, his tone mocking. "That is the sweetest little smile. And just for me?"

He touched an index finger to the corner of her mouth, lingered longer than was wise before dropping his hand and picking up on his mission. "Only one reason I can think of for you to be this mellow. Got yourself sloshed on champagne, didn't you?"

The soft chocolate of her eyes hardened to blackened cinders. Her sexy kitten smile tightened to a guard dog snarl. In the instant before the transformation, however, anger wasn't the first emotion that clouded her face.

An aching disappointment had flickered there. And for that moment, for an eternity, so did something else. A vulnerability as unexpected as it was heartbreaking had surfaced in this woman who showed no fear. And in that moment, he'd felt less of a man.

Both the disappointment and the vulnerability dissipated as quickly as they'd appeared. So quickly, in fact, that he wondered if he'd just imagined them. He would have sworn he'd imagined them, if he hadn't felt the guilt slamming into his gut like a heavyweight's fist.

He'd hurt her. He hadn't meant to. Hadn't known he was capable. Or that he would feel this much remorse because of it.

She didn't waste any time recovering.

"Sloshed?" she repeated in a tone laced with the acid he was comfortable with but which didn't quite conceal the hit he'd given her pride. "Well then, I'll bet that would explain why I'm about to do this."

Her smile was as flat as stale soda as she grabbed a full glass of champagne from a nearby tray. Her intent was as clear as an angel about to ditch her halo when she curled her fingers over his belt buckle, glared into his eyes and emptied the contents of the glass inside the front of his pants.

Three

The next morning Maddie bent over her potter's wheel, worked the foot treadle and leveled all of her frustration and humiliation on a poor defenseless mound of clay. It was another Clay that came to mind, though, when she punched it with her fist and set about shaping it the way she wanted. She had almost as much luck with the wet, cold lump as she did keeping her thoughts about the wet warm mouth of the banana boy at bay.

After fifteen minutes of fragmented concentration and no productivity, she gave up. Shoulders slumped, she stared dismally out the back window of her studio and tried to talk last night away.

"It never happened," she told Maxwell, her calico tomcat who accompanied her to work each day. "I did not stand there at the party like a thirteen-year-old bubblegummer and make moon eyes at Clay James. I did not plant myself smack in front of him and invite him to kiss me.

And I absolutely did not buckle like a broken table leg when he read my mind and his devastatingly sensual mouth twisted into a mocking sneer before accusing me of being sloshed.''

She stopped, waited, listened for absolution from Maxwell in the ringing silence. The cat just blinked. And, unfortunately, repeating the events aloud only slapped her humiliation right back in her face.

She rolled the stiffness from her shoulders and let out a disgusted breath. What on earth had she been thinking? Maybe Clay was right. Maybe it had been the champagne. At least that would give her an excuse for why she'd actually tried to flirt with him.

Forearms propped heavily on her thighs, she made an absent poke at the clay with the tip of her finger.

"Nice try, Brannigan," she muttered giving up on sympathy from the cat as he curled up in a halo of sunlight spilling across the floor, "but you weren't *sloshed,* as the man so eloquently put it."

What she'd been was curious. What she'd been was intrigued by Garrett's suggestions, aroused by certain memories—and captivated by a pair of stunning blue eyes, the subtle shift of awareness on his part and the promise of pleasures a man like Clay could incite.

"Nope. Definitely not tipsy," she conceded, shaking her head in disgust. It was worse. She was insane. And the very worst part of that was that he knew it. Just like he knew what she'd been thinking and wanting and wondering about.

"Well, that's what you get for dabbling near the lunatic fringes of animal lust," she muttered, and started pedaling again in earnest. "You set out to satisfy a curiosity, and you ended up with a bruise to your pride roughly the size of the Tetons."

Not exactly a fair trade, but it was the one she'd made

and she was stuck with it. Now all she had do was figure out how to live through the construction of her gallery without letting him know how badly his reaction had hurt her.

With a mental kick in the butt, she tucked back into her work—then gave up five minutes later when she pedaled so hard the clay jumped off the wheel and slammed with a smacking thud into the far wall.

Maxwell, so named because he was as faithful as her favorite brand of coffee in waking her up every morning, raised his head, watched the clay slide down the wall, then went back to sleep.

Across town, in his office at the James Construction Company, Clay stared at a materials list for a late-fall project. The fact that it was close to noon and he'd been scowling over the same page for the past hour didn't do much to improve his mood.

He was still hung up on last night. It had been a first-class disaster that had started with his "Chiquita Banana" performance. Maddie's baptism of his fly at the party afterward should have been the topper. Not so. It was Veronica's not-so-subtle inquiry about where their relationship was headed and her subsequent suggestion that he take his "let's not rush into anything" reply and stuff it, along with his head, into a bucket of horse manure, that finished things off nicely.

One thing about it: he'd sure seen a side of Veronica he'd never seen before. A part of him was relieved to know there was something more substantial than cake recipes behind those limpid blue eyes. Another part, however, was shocked that the substance was so toxic.

Not that he blamed her for getting mad. He'd been sending out some pretty strong signals lately—commitment signals. He wasn't even sure why he suddenly had this panicked urge to back away.

It was confusing as hell. He was ready to settle down. He wanted Veronica to be the one—had been thinking she *was* the one—that he wanted to settle down with. Yet one smile, one sexy, smoldering, tipsy little smile from the guru of irritation, and he was second-guessing his second guesses.

It had to stop.

For the fourth time that morning he told himself to send Veronica flowers and a note of apology.

For the fourth time he never quite got himself to do it. As a matter of fact, when he really thought about it, he was relatively certain he wouldn't be sending flowers or phone calls or anything else Veronica's way ever again.

The thought should have bothered him more. And it might have if he hadn't finally admitted that, while he liked Veronica well enough, he didn't love her. He'd loved the idea of loving her, of getting married, of starting a family. But the God's honest truth was that he didn't love her and he'd only been fooling himself into thinking that he could. No, he wouldn't be calling Veronica again.

Before he got too philosophical about why he was so willing to let go of a certain, lasting relationship, his mind veered off in another direction. He start thinking about Maddie again and how she'd looked, all soft eyed, and sweetly inviting. And of the look in her eyes when he'd panicked and resorted to his old standby tactic of ticking her off.

He slumped back in his chair and tossed the materials list onto his desk. Cupping his jaw in his palm, he stared into space and pictured Maddie's face when he'd accused her of having too much to drink. The sudden but fleeting pain in her eyes had made a part of him want to punch his own lights out.

He hadn't meant to hurt her. And he sure as hell hadn't planned on losing sleep over the fact that he had. For pity's sake, this was old hat to both of them. This was business as usual. They always went at each other.

But he'd never felt mean before.

He passed a paper clip back and forth between his fingers. And he'd never, ever felt the weight of guilt for causing her pain—no matter how short-lived.

He didn't like it. Not any of it. And he particularly didn't like all the time he was wasting thinking about her.

Shoving out of his chair, he stalked to the window, crossed his arms over his chest and stuffed balled fists under his armpits. Hell, she's the one who should be apologizing. She'd embarrassed the hell out of him with that trick she'd pulled with the champagne. And he was the one who was going to bear the brunt of those damn banana jokes for months to come, too. He didn't dare forget that he had Maddie Brannigan to thank for all of it.

And for his sleepless night and unproductive morning.

And for this sick feeling in his gut every time he flashed on a picture of her face when he'd given her the verbal equivalent of a right hook instead of the kiss they'd both been in danger of taking.

All right. Enough was enough. So he'd hurt her feelings. He still stood by his assessment of why she'd been giving him a taste of the sex kitten instead of the mad dog. If he didn't, then the situation was just that much more untenable.

It *was* the champagne. The champagne had softened the snapping, pepper brown of her eyes to a rich, liquid chocolate. The champagne had painted the dusky blush on her cheeks. Most notably, however, it was the champagne, not some latent change of heart, that had mellowed her mood beyond grudging tolerance, beyond even a temporary truce, to a misty sort of sexuality. A steamy deviation to flirtation.

Fool woman.

He stalked back to his desk, figuring he'd taken care of

explaining what had motivated her. But he ended up staring into space again trying to sort out where *he'd* been coming from and why after a lifetime of wanting to shut that smart mouth of hers, all he could think about now—all he could fantasize about—was kissing it.

Two weeks later on a warm September afternoon, Maddie was itching for a good fight. She knew just the man who could give it to her, too, if she could get him to stand still long enough to let her tie into him.

Construction dust tickled her toes through her sandals as she made her way across the gallery's building site looking for Clay. She found him standing fifteen feet up on a scaffold, stripped to the waist. A healthy layer of dust and perspiration coated the glistening tan of his bare back and showcased an impressive flex of muscle.

There was a certain and substantial pleasure seeing Clay James all hot and sweaty, she decided. Not, she assured herself, because even dirty and sweaty, Clay James was powerfully pleasing to the eye. Not even because she liked the idea of his usual image—pressed jeans, tucked and tidy Western shirt and polished boots—being a little messed and muddied. Looking like this wasn't a break from his routine. Just like Garrett, Clay dug in and worked with his crew. He was a hands-on contractor, at home in a business suit or a layer of construction dust.

She liked seeing him this way today because it meant he was busting his taut little buns just for her. It was strictly a power trip. For the duration of the construction, she called the shots. And she liked that arrangement just fine.

Yet as the sun glinted off the polished bronze of his skin and the steady pounding of his hammer delineated and defined the strength and grace of the muscle beneath, she had to dig deep to remember why a working relationship was the only relationship they could ever have.

It was because she had perspective now, that's why, she told herself as she brushed some sawdust from her ankle-length gray leggings, then arranged her pink middy T-shirt so the boat neck was squared on her shoulders again. It had taken a full fourteen days, but she'd finally managed to put things back into neat little slots after the night of the cast party. The memory of that night remained, a sharp slap of reality right across her face, but she couldn't change what had happened.

Talk about a hard lesson learned. Thanks to Garrett's suggestions and her overblown memories, she'd actually been thinking about Clay in terms of other than getting even and paying back. She'd been thinking in terms of romance and attraction and—well, it didn't matter what else. It didn't matter that Clay and Veronica were no longer a couple, either. She wasn't thinking that way anymore.

The upshot was that she'd learned one colossal, heart-wrenching lesson. He had the power to make her feel vulnerable. For that she would never forgive him. For that matter, she'd never forgive herself for letting it happen. And she would never let him see that less-than-invincible side of her again. Add to that the way he'd been acting the past two weeks, and she had enough motivation to keep things in perspective through the next millennium.

It was going to take both of them to level the playing field again, however, and he wasn't pulling his weight. She'd finally decided that the way to get back to business was to pick up where they'd veered off course. For the past week she'd tried to needle him, outmaneuver him and generally irritate the heck out of him. That, after all, was status quo.

The man, however, wouldn't give her the satisfaction of status quo. What he gave her instead was the repeated sight of his neatly packed Wranglers walking away from her.

And when he wasn't walking away, he was avoiding her like she carried the doomsday virus.

It did not sit well. As the building project progressed and she saw minor adjustments that she wanted to rile him about, he'd bite back his anger, neatly refer her to Garrett and exit stage left.

She'd gotten his message. Loud and strong. He wasn't just blowing her off the way he usually did when she annoyed him. It was more like he didn't even have it in him to feel annoyed. Like it wasn't worth his effort. And somehow, his total lack of emotion was more disconcerting than if he'd bellowed at her for being a pest. She felt uncomfortably adrift because of it.

Well, she'd had enough. She had far more interesting things to do than wonder what his new attitude was all about. And she would never make the mistake again of letting that pretty package make her heart or her head go all mushy.

So she'd made a mistake. She'd let Garrett's suggestion, a lot of sensual memory, and an itsy-bitsy case of melancholy head her in the absolute wrong direction.

She was over it. It was past and her head was back on straight for the present. He needed to get his back on straight, too.

That's why she'd come looking for him today. To get right in his face and force him to prove to her and to himself that it was back to business-as-usual between them. She was willing to be tormented, bullied and badgered. She was also willing to be the tormentor, bullier and badgerer. What she was not willing to be was ignored. Not by him. Not one minute longer.

Marching up to the base of the scaffolding, she shaded her eyes against the sun's glare with the shield of her hand. "Clay—can I talk to you?"

He quickly covered his surprise at seeing her there by

sparing her a bored glance before going back to his hammering. "You might not have noticed. I'm a little busy."

"I won't keep you long," she sputtered, immediately incensed by his ready dismissal. "And I really need to talk to you."

With a deep, weary breath, he turned, stared impassively down at her, then reluctantly hooked his hammer in a loop on his tool belt. "So talk."

She expelled a long, tolerant sigh and stayed the course. "Could you please come down here? Five minutes. That's all I need, and I'd just as soon not shout my way through this conversation."

Again he favored her with a vacant look before he tugged off his hard hat and wiped the sweat from his brow with a swipe of his forearm. A long moment passed before he finally gave in and climbed down the scaffolding.

His heavy work boots had no sooner hit the ground with a little puff of dust than he reached for a thermal water jug. He unscrewed the lid and tipped it back.

She didn't want to be, she sure as the world shouldn't be, but she was mesmerized by the sight. Sweat trickled down his temples and neck, matting the hair at his nape in spiky, damp curls. The taut cords in his throat convulsed with every swallow as he downed half the contents in long, thirsty gulps. A heavy dusting of dark curls covered his broad chest then narrowed to a thin silken arrow beyond the washboard leanness of his belly before disappearing under the low-slung waist of his jeans.

The sight of him that way, all messy and sexy and sweaty, had her fidgeting with her hair like a schoolgirl and working up a thirst of her own.

"Five minutes," he said after setting aside the Thermos. With a glance at his watch, he propped gloved fists impatiently on his hips and waited.

His clipped, gruff reminder was all it took to snap her

out of her little erotic tailspin and match his no-nonsense glare.

"Many thanks for the audience, oh great one whose time is more precious than gold," she muttered, overplaying the dutiful supplicant to his superior, put-upon male.

He gave her a slow, bored blink. "You want to talk or smart off? And now you're down to four and a half minutes."

Okay. So an adult exchange was out of the question. She'd improvise despite Garrett's warnings that ever since the party following the variety show, Clay had been as touchy as a rattler roused from his hidey-hole. Accepting that he was in one of his moods today, she got straight to the point. And straight to the business of riling him out of his calm, controlled aloofness.

Lucky for her, she knew the perfect way to go about it.

"I think there was a little misunderstanding on the blue-prints," she said baldly.

His blue eyes momentarily darkened with deadly malice before he tamped down on his temper and leveled her a dispassionate look. "A misunderstanding? And that would be a misunderstanding on whose part?"

"Yours?" she suggested, baiting him with a wide, innocent smile.

His jaw clenched reflexively, temporarily. "Let me see if I've got this right. I drew the blueprints and yet you figure I don't understand them."

While his calculated calm was underscored with irritation, his mild reaction was a little more unsettling than she'd like to admit. And a little harder to deal with than the yelling she'd been working for. Hoping her discomfort didn't show, she shifted her wandering T-shirt back onto her shoulders, crossed her arms over her chest, let them drop, crossed them again. "Well, I think it's more a matter of you didn't understand how I visualized things."

He closed his eyes, tightened his lips, then shook his head in disbelief. "Then—and please correct me if I'm wrong," he said, his words suddenly dripping sarcasm, "wouldn't that mean that *you* misunderstood something?"

"Regardless," she said, shrugging off the accuracy of his logic, "this is not quite the way I had envisioned the setup."

Very slowly, very deliberately, he raised his hand and rubbed at the spot above his left eye where she'd noticed a frenzied and frantic little twitching had begun.

"We talked about this, Maddie. I believe we talked about it a lot. In fact, I was very specific. I told you up front— several times—that if you wanted changes, you needed to make them in the planning stage—not the construction stage."

"I realize that," she said, feeling her confidence build now that his carefully modulated voice had escalated ever so slightly, "and I appreciate your stand on that issue, but—"

"Hold it right there. There are no buts. In case you hadn't noticed, the entire building is framed up and the roof and exterior walls are in place."

"And looking really, really good, by the way," she interjected in a tone so deliberately placating it guaranteed a rise in his body temperature. "The exterior is great! Fantastic. It's just that there are a few minor adjustments on the interior that need to be made."

"A few—minor adjustments." He'd raised his big hands and crossed them heavily over his chest. His chin jutted belligerently toward her. And, if she didn't miss her guess, his jaws were now clenched so tightly the enamel on his teeth was in danger of being ground to powder.

"Just a few," she assured him, trying a smile that was about as effective as pouring a thimbleful of water on a blazing grass fire. "And I'm sure Garrett wouldn't think any of them would be a very big deal."

"Oh, well—" he waved a hand through the air "—if you're so sure Garrett wouldn't have a problem, why didn't you talk to him?"

"Because he said I needed to talk to you."

His expression was as hard as his hammer. "Fine. Now we've talked. No changes. I'm going back to work."

Then he turned back toward the scaffolding, leaving her all revved up and no one to snipe at.

This was not the way it was supposed to work. He was supposed to rant and rave, and she was supposed to yell right back and then everything would get back to normal.

He thought he was just going to walk away? Not in this lifetime. They'd been that far from a good old-fashioned shouting match, and she was primed for action.

"Just like that?" she exclaimed, snagging his arm and stopping him. "You won't even listen to what I want changed?"

He glared from her face to the hand clutching his arm. She felt the burn of both his skin, hot under her fingers, and his eyes, blazing under hooded brows.

"Just like that." The leather of his work gloves was soft and supple as he pried her fingers from his arm. "It's only fair, don't you think, since you obviously didn't listen to me when I told you there would be no changes once we got started."

"Oh, for heaven's sake. You'd think I was asking you to rebuild the White House. All I want is a minor—"

"You signed a contract," he said, cutting her off.

"Yeah, I did. I signed a contract to pay you a lot of money to build a gallery for me. Those are hard-earned dollars, and they ought to buy me a little latitude."

She wasn't sure when she'd started shouting or when he'd lost his carefully modulated control and started shouting back. She wasn't even sure when their discussion had escalated from baiting to battling and her own temper had gotten the best of her. She only knew it had. And his snarling reply shoved her over the edge to hornet's-nest mad. And hot damn, it felt good.

"How's this for latitude?" he barked, completely forgetting he wasn't supposed to let her get to him. "You want changes? Here's a big one. I quit. Now you can go hire yourself a new contractor to make the other ones for you."

That skidded her to an abrupt stop. But only for a second. "Oh, no you don't. I hired you to do the job and that's who's going to do it."

He lowered his head to within inches of hers. "Then get out of my face."

"Or what?" she shot back.

He set that impossible granite jaw and glared through narrowed eyes. "Or you'll be sorry that you didn't."

"Was that a threat?" she snapped, right on his heels when he turned again to climb back up the scaffold. "That sounded like a threat."

His booted foot hit the first ladder rung. "That works out real nice, then, because that's exactly what it was."

"Oh, that is really rich. The big bad cowboy is threatening the little woman. Well, come on, then, tough guy. If it makes you feel better, give it your best shot. What's it gonna be? You want to punch me out? Maybe blacken my—"

She never finished her taunt. He spun around and came after her so fast she yelped, then nearly tripped over her own feet trying to scurry away.

He wasn't about to let her go anywhere. Snagging her by both shoulders, he dragged her up against him so hard that the words and the breath whooshed out of her with one sharp, involuntary gasp.

"How about I just shut your mouth instead?"

"Wh-what do you think you're doing?" she stammered, wondering if she'd pushed him too far.

"I'm giving you what you asked for. Exactly what you asked for," he snarled as he knotted a gloved fist in her hair and pressed her back against an outside wall. "And don't think—not for one minute—that you didn't."

A trickle of arousal dovetailed with fear and inched down her spine. There was hostility in the eyes that threatened her, intent in the hard set of his mouth. And there was anger, unleashed and unrepentant in the hard crush of the body that pressed her deeper against the building.

But above it all, simmering like the heated waters of a thermal pool, bubbling like the cauldron of a warlock's brew, was something much more volatile: arousal. Pure. Primitive. Dangerous. As reckless as the wild thunder of her heart. As stunning as the storm brewing in his eyes as he lowered his head and slanted his mouth over hers.

She tried to scream out a protest. To deny that this was happening. To remind him, for heaven's sake, that this was not what he was supposed to be doing.

He was supposed to be mad, yes. Like old times. Like comfortable old times when they'd snipe and volley and both of them would feel triumphant and ticked off at the same time.

He was not supposed to kiss her. He most definitely was not supposed to kiss her like she was the saving drink of water to a man dying of thirst. And he was absolutely not supposed to alternately gentle then ravage her with hungry bites and teasing nips and dizzying sensual forays inside her mouth with his tongue.

And she, she was positively not supposed to melt like licorice under a summer sun and let him do it.

But he did. And she did until she was stunned into ac-quiescence, seduced into responding when he groaned from deep in his throat and took her under again. And then again.

With a surrendering sigh, she wrapped her arms around his neck, pressed herself against his heat and rode with the sultry crush of chest to breast, teeth to tongue, heartbeat to heartbeat.

On a peripheral level she was aware of the breeze stirring the dust beneath their feet and lifting the curls around her face. Of the sunlight infusing the shadows of the scaffolding and lending its baking heat to the blaze of the fire he'd ignited. She was aware of the unforgiving wall of her gallery at her back, of the unyielding male body pinning her there, of his scent, his sweat, and an anger that had transmuted to a dark, carnal craving.

It was the cat calls that finally brought her back from that sharp, sweet edge of desire. It was the applause and the look of pure, male dominance on his face as he slowly pulled away from her that reminded her where she was, what he'd done, and reloaded her anger like the slam of a shell in the chamber of a shotgun.

The building crew had not only been an appreciative audience for his little show of male supremacy but they'd witnessed her bending to his will. Desire dove beneath humiliation, but she'd be damned if she'd let him see it.

Blinking back tears, she stared him straight in the eye and drew her arm back for a blow she hoped would knock him into next week. "You son of a—"

With maddening ease, he snagged her wrist mid-swing and twisted her arm behind her back.

"Temper, temper, Matilda," he taunted, then hauled her up into his arms and marched across the lot. "When are you ever going to learn that temper of yours buys you nothing but trouble?"

"Put me down." She ground out the words one caustic syllable at a time.

"With pleasure," he replied just as acidly.

Then he dumped her without apology or remorse into a wheelbarrow full of wet cement.

She gasped then sucked in a strangled breath as the thick, cold mix oozed around her like quicksand.

"Don't bother firing me," he added as an afterthought as she sat on her butt, waist-deep in the mucky gray sludge, her mouth and her eyes wide open in disbelief. "I quit."

And then he left her to the wary but amused stares of the crew while she hurled handfuls of sloppy concrete and a string of blistering curses at his departing back.

Four

"It's gotten out of hand, Clayton." Maya James Bradford, perched on the corner of Garrett's desk, frowned at her middle son with typical mother's concern. "You and Maddie have been at each other for years, but that stunt you pulled yesterday..." She shook her head in dismay. The end of her thought may have remained unspoken, but her message came across loud and clear.

Clay scratched his jaw and walked to the window. She was right, of course. This business with Maddie *had* gotten out of hand. He'd been cursing himself for a fool ever since his little performance on the building site yesterday.

Not that he regretted dumping her into the cement. She'd had that coming. She'd been spoiling for a fight and he'd given her one. What he'd regretted was what had happened just before that.

He still couldn't believe he'd kissed her. Publicly. Passionately. And he'd liked it. A lot. That's the part he was sorry about. He'd been struggling to shake off the effects of that kiss ever since.

When he realized his mother was still waiting for an explanation and no other defense was forthcoming, he mumbled a surly, "She started it," then realized how childish he sounded.

Maya rolled her eyes. "Oh, please. Will you listen to yourself? You sound like a six-year-old. Next you'll be accusing her of stealing your candy."

From his seat behind his desk, Garrett tried unsuccessfully to camouflage a chuckle behind a manufactured cough.

Maya turned her dark eyes his way. "This is not funny," she scolded, then in that way she had, managed to let both of her sons know she loved them but was disappointed in their actions.

"We've got to initiate some damage control," she went on. "Now I think Emma's convinced Maddie not to press charges for harassment and assault, but she's still holding firm on banning you from the job site, Clay."

"Fine with me," he said stubbornly. "The more distance between me and Matilda the Hun the better off I'll be."

"Yeah, well, it's not fine with me," Garrett chimed in. "It's a big project—and since you masterminded it, little brother, I need you to help finish it up."

"Why don't we just cut our losses and let her hire a new contractor to finish the work?"

Maya narrowed her eyes at Clay's suggestion. After all these years, she still had the ability to make him feel sheepish.

"Because this is our project," she pointed out unnecessarily. "And because we don't leave customers in the lurch."

"Fine," Clay said, knowing he sounded like that belligerent six-year-old again but not caring. He snagged his Stetson from the hat rack and headed out of Garrett's office, pausing with a broad hand clasped on the door frame. "We'll finish it. And in record time. Just keep her off the building site, and I'll work twenty-four hours a day to get it done."

Both Maya and Garrett let out pent-up breaths when Clay slammed the door behind him.

"Ideas?" Maya asked hopefully into the thick silence that had settled.

Garrett pinched his jaw, considering an idea he and Emma had been contemplating for some time concerning Clay and Maddie. "Maybe. What I've got in mind will take a little contriving. But it might be our only shot."

"Then take it. Anything to get through this and not lose credibility in the business."

"The credibility, we can salvage. I know Maddie. She's just blowing smoke and venting steam with her threat to press charges. She'll settle down on that count. It's the loss of blood that worries me." His quick grin was both devious and secretive.

"Whatever you're planning," Maya cut in quickly, a look of reluctant guilt washing over her face, "I don't want to know about it. Not one word. What I don't know can't implicate me, and I lost enough sleep over my culpability when you boys plotted to kidnap Emma. I don't want to be a party to another scenario as potentially explosive as that one."

Garrett picked up the phone. "You might want to leave, then," he suggested with a sly grin as he punched in Jesse's pager number, "because you definitely don't want to hear this conversation."

"Say no more." Maya scooted off Garrett's desk and headed for the door. "I'm sure I have something to do. Logan must need me or miss me or want me for something."

"That, I don't doubt," Garrett said, pleased that his mother continued to be so happy in her recent marriage to Logan Bradford. She'd been alone for fifteen long years after their father had died. She was still a vital, beautiful woman and deserved all the happiness Bradford could give her.

What she didn't need any more of was trouble from any of her boys. "Mom," he said, stopping her as she reached the door. He replaced the receiver and waited for Jesse to answer his page. "Don't worry. We'll make sure there's no gunplay."

With a pained look, Maya left, asking the good Lord to save her from her smart-mouthed children and to forgive her for turning Garrett and Jesse loose on Maddie and Clay.

The end, she prayed, would justify the scheme. Those two were in love with each other. She just knew it. But if they didn't get the chance to sort through an inordinate amount of baggage they'd dragged with them from childhood, they were going to seriously maim each other—emotionally for certain, and physically too if their last little encounter was any indication—before they ever figured it out.

Maddie cast a mellow look at the forest surrounding her, Wind River gurgling a few yards distant and the mountains rising above it all. "I'm really glad I let you talk me into coming along this weekend."

Emma smiled at Maddie before diverting her gaze back to Sara Jane. The little girl was busy constructing a fort with rocks and twigs near the riverbank. "You needed a break. So did I. And Sara has been curious about the cabin where Daddy took Mommy to make her smile again."

A soft, reflective glow washed over Emma's features. Maddie knew Emma was thinking back to the week she and Garrett had spent here healing their marriage and learning to trust each other again. It was a contented look. A satisfied look that Maddie understood was private and special. She wasn't sure what all had happened here between Garrett and Emma this past summer. And she would never ask. It was an intimate and special time for the two of them.

She understood the magical results of their time in this mountain retreat, though. Emma hadn't looked this happy in years.

"I'm glad everything worked out with you and Garrett, Em," she said softly.

Emma smiled. "Me, too. And now, what better way to get back in touch with nature and bond as women than with a weekend retreat to the infamous James boys' cabin."

Maddie snorted indelicately and shoved the sleeves of her baggy red sweater up to her elbows. "Yeah, there is something cleansing about knowing we're the first women to go solo in a for-men-only domain."

"Just like pioneers," Emma added in agreement. "It's beautiful here, isn't it?"

Perched on a downed pine trunk beside Emma, Maddie inhaled deeply of the scent of mountain forest and crisp clean air. She took a long, slow look around her. Yes, it was definitely beautiful here. The Wind River, running clear and shallow in early fall, snaked around bend after bend, following a natural path that it cut out of the valley. The jagged mountain range in the background, though commonplace to someone who had grown up near the Tetons, still held uncommon value and breathtaking beauty for her.

After spending just one day and night here, Maddie understood why this particular spot and the cabin Jonathan James had built for his family almost thirty years ago held such import in the brothers' hearts. Those of them who *had* hearts, she clarified mentally, as Clay's handsome, arrogant face came to mind.

"It was nice of Garrett to suggest that we girls take a

minisabbatical here," she conceded, keeping her thoughts about Clay to herself.

"It wasn't just up to Garrett," Emma reminded her. "Clay had to give his blessing, too, just like Jesse did."

"Childhood pact and all that," Maddie said, remembering Garrett's account of how, when they were boys spending summer vacations in their mountain stronghold, they'd declared it a "men-only territory" and that the only way the tradition could be broken was by consensus of all three brothers.

"I'm surprised Clay went for it," Maddie mused aloud, "supreme, selfish, male chauvinist pig that he is and all."

Emma grinned at the throw-away venom in Maddie's statement. "He's not really such a bad guy, Maddie. I think you know that."

"What I know is that he's a perpetual pain in my side. I also know that if you hadn't assured me that he won't be requiring my undying gratitude for the rest of my life, I wouldn't be here now."

"He won't. He knows the getaway is more for Sara Jane and me to experience a taste of what Garrett and the brothers shared as children. And I think that deep down, Clay was relieved you came along as an extra pair of eyes and hands to make sure Sara doesn't get into trouble."

Another snort. "Yeah. Like he takes a lot of stock in *my* abilities."

"More than he'd ever admit," Emma assured her.

With a roll of her eyes, Maddie let the subject of Clay James drop. She didn't want to talk about him. She didn't even want to think about him. Because if she did, she had to think about that kiss. And that kiss was—well, that kiss was something she needed to forget. Trouble was, her subconscious wouldn't let her. At night—oh, Lord, especially at night—the memory infused her thoughts and her body like a July sun heated pale skin. First it warmed, then it burned, and then it left her alone in the night to deal with the fever that settled much farther than surface deep.

Aware, suddenly, that the memory had taken over again, she made herself think about all the work Garrett and Jesse had gone to, to get them up here for their little getaway.

Garrett had laid all the groundwork, completed the plans. Jesse had come home to help him stock the cabin with food, lay in a supply of wood for their evening fires, make sure the generator and water system were working before packing the three of them up here by horseback Friday afternoon. And it was Garrett, along with Jesse, who had left them before dark that same day.

Satisfied they were well settled, the men had ridden away with a promise to return Sunday afternoon to lead the way back out of the valley and over the mountains. Once down the trail, they'd load the horses into the waiting trailer and make the two-hour drive back to Jackson.

Lords knows, they needed to be guided out. Maddie didn't know about Emma, but she freely admitted she had the tracking instincts of a rock. She'd been known to lose her car in grocery store parking lots and in clearly marked parking ramps. Finding her way out of these mountains on her own wasn't even a remote possibility.

In the meantime, however, feeling secure in Garrett and Jesse's eventual return, she wasn't concerned about finding her way back. Frankly, she wasn't concerned about much of anything but whiling away this glorious sunshiny Saturday with her best friend and the child whose heart had won hers the moment she was born.

"She's so beautiful," Maddie said as she watched the sunlight play with the highlights in Sara's chestnut hair.

Emma followed her gaze. "Sometimes it's hard to fully embrace the fact that Garrett and I made something so perfect."

Understanding completely, and wondering, with a bit of

melancholy, if she would ever know first-hand the sweet, precious experience of motherhood, Maddie just nodded.

Silence settled like a calm breeze then suddenly felt full, as if something important had been left unsaid.

Maddie turned to Emma to see that she was watching her with a secret little smile on her face.

"What?" she asked, suddenly breathless with expectancy but not knowing why.

Emma's smile became radiant as she reached for Maddie's hand. "I'm pregnant."

For a moment all Maddie could do was stare. Then the sting of joyous tears filled her eyes. "Oh, Em. That's so...that's so wonderful! When? And how are you? And does Garrett know?" The questions tumbled out, one on top of the other, making them both laugh and tear up at the same time as they shared a long, affectionate hug.

"March. And I'm fine. And yes, Garrett knows and he's ecstatic."

"Oh, my gosh! This is so great! But...oh, wait. Should you be up here? I mean, the horseback ride and all. Is it a problem?"

Maddie's concern was well founded. Emma had miscarried, a little over two years ago. It had been devastating to both Emma and Garrett and ultimately had even affected their marriage.

"No problem," Emma assured her quickly. "Doctor says there's no reason to be concerned about the danger of another miscarriage. I'm healthy. The baby's healthy. The fresh air and exercise can be nothing but good for both of us."

Reassured, Maddie couldn't stop grinning. "Does Sara know?"

Emma shook her head and glanced in Sara's direction. "No. We want to wait until I'm showing before we tell her. No sense in getting her wound up about it too soon.

In the meantime, we told Maya and Logan and my mother last week. Garrett's telling the brothers as we speak.''

The rest of the afternoon they chattered excitedly about redoing the nursery, about Emma and Garrett's choice to wait until the birth to find out if the baby was a boy or a girl and about a dozen other inconsequential but vastly important details surrounding the pregnancy and birth.

And later that night, after the three of them had cooked plump, juicy hot dogs over the fire in the fireplace, stuffed themselves with s'mores until they'd had to change from their jeans to sweat pants and finally settled into their beds, Maddie stared into the dark.

Happy for her friend.

Grateful for their friendship.

Battling tears she hated herself for needing to shed.

She tried so hard not to be anything but grateful. Instead, she felt the ugly beginnings of envy creep in and blacken her good intentions.

She couldn't help it. She wanted what Emma had. She wanted the love of a good man. She wanted a child. Her child. To love. To teach and nurture. To hold against her breast and share with the man who helped make it happen.

Moonlight spilled through the window in the loft bedroom and across the bed where she lay, diluting the darkness, isolating her in a tumble of moonbeams and solitude. And in this warm oak-hewn cabin she shared with her best friend and her child, she'd never felt more alone or miserably self-pitying in her life.

''Will you quit grumbling and just bite the proverbial bullet?''

Clay glared at Garrett's back as they traversed a particularly tricky leg of the trail up the mountain. ''If I wanted to bite bullets, I'd have joined the carnival as a novelty act. And if I'd have wanted to ride all the way to the cabin just to turn around and guide the shrew of the century back to town so she can embed herself as a burr under my saddle again, I'd have volunteered for the job.''

"All right, already. I get the message. Believe me. If I could have found someone else to help me bring the girls and all the gear it took to get them through the weekend back home, I wouldn't be listening to you griping.''

Clay snorted. "Leave it to Jesse to bail out when you needed him.''

"It couldn't be helped. He had a change of plans.''

Actually, it was a change Garrett had orchestrated with Jesse's willing assistance. With luck, Clay would never find out that tidbit of information. Making sure Jesse wasn't around was what made Clay's trek to the cabin necessary. And that, after all, was what this little setup was all about.

Clay gave another disgusted snort and rode on. "Don't expect me to be civil.''

"I can, without reservation, say that that thought never crossed my mind,'' Garrett muttered drily and wondered for the umpteenth time if he dared follow through with his plan. Telling himself things couldn't possibly get any worse, he set his hat tighter on his head and decided to stay the course.

And may heaven help us all if this doesn't work.

Once Clay and Garrett reached the cabin, it took some planned confusion, some devious contriving and some downright calculated risks on both Emma and Garrett's part, but finally, everything fell into place.

With Emma running everything from interference to decoy, she managed to send Maddie on foot to find the jacket Sara must have left by the river. At the same time, Clay played right into their hands. Counting on his religious avoidance of Maddie, Garrett sent him after the same jacket—but in the totally opposite direction.

That critical part of the plan accomplished, Emma left the note they'd written in preparation for this moment on the table in the cabin while Garrett rounded up all five horses. Then, with the stealth and swiftness of the James Gang of old on the run from the law, the three of them hightailed it out of the valley, out of sight and out of shouting distance.

It was do or die time for Clay James and Maddie Brannigan. Without horses they were as good as stuck here until Garrett came back for them a week from today. Oh sure, Clay could walk out if he had a mind to spend a solid day on foot and then take his chances hitching a ride back to Jackson when he did stumble out of the mountains. Maddie, however, was another story. She was a tenderfoot from way back. Garrett was counting on Clay to have the innate decency not to drag her on a long hike or to leave her to fend for herself. He was counting on a lot of things—like two stubborn, strong-willed people figuring out that they could fire something other than anger in each other's direction if they'd just give it a chance.

As they crested the ridge at a hard gallop, Garrett noted the thunderheads rolling into the valley they'd left behind. He sent a silent thank-you skyward and stepped up their pace so they could stay ahead of the storm. A good old-fashioned soaker was the perfect incentive for Clay and Maddie to bow to the elements and commit themselves to settling in.

Beside him, Emma murmured her own prayer heavenward. She prayed that when Garrett went back for them seven days from now, not only would Clay and Maddie both be in one piece, but that they would have discovered that essential element that everyone around them already knew.

After a fifteen-minute hike to the spot where Emma was sure Sara Jane had left her jacket and another half hour searching in vain, Maddie decided she'd been sent on a wild-goose chase. She smiled, silently thanking her friend for her discretion. Emma, sweet soul, knew how difficult it was for Maddie to be around Clay. The jacket diversion was Emma's way of keeping distance between them.

With a promise to thank Emma for her thoughtfulness when she saw her, she began the hike back to the cabin. Normally, given her sense of direction, she wouldn't have braved the trek alone. They'd picnicked at this spot three times this weekend, however, and she felt comfortable finding her way back. It was with no small amount of pride that she did just that.

As she broke clear of the forest, and the cabin came into sight, however, her pride was sullied by a little frisson of unease. Where there should have been activity, there was a total lack of it. Where there should have been voices, there was a ringing, empty silence.

And where five horses should have been waiting, saddled up and carrying full packs, there was only one man. One extremely angry man.

Clay stood, a lone figure, his feet planted wide, his back ramrod straight, a sheet of paper crushed in a tightly clenched fist. The icy glare he shot her from beneath the shadowed brim of his Stetson as he turned away from the distant mountain peak and toward the sound of her approach could be summed up in one concise four-letter word. Fury.

"They did what?" The hard, clipped words exploded from her, punctuated by an oath, when Clay told her that Garrett and Emma had ridden out of the valley and left them there.

Clay uttered another crisp, concise curse and kicked hard at the dirt beneath his feet. He jerked his hat from his head, dragged a hand roughly through his hair then resettled the Stetson with a hard tug before shoving the crumpled note into her hand. "Read it yourself."

With wild eyes Maddie smoothed out the paper. Then she tried to read the words through a panic mottled by the red-hot anger pounding behind her eyes.

The note was short, to the point, and devastating:

> We love you both. However, we can't stand seeing you go at each other anymore. You've got a week to work something out. Just don't add to our guilt for tricking you this way by drawing blood. Maddie— we'll take care of the gallery and Maxwell. Clay— Garrett will handle things at work.

With a squeal of disbelief, Maddie read it again then zeroed in on the final line of Emma and Garrett's message:

> This valley is special. So are both of you. Let the magic and the moments work for you the way it did for Garrett and me. Garrett will be back for both of you in seven days.

"Oh, my God," she whispered, a sick knot forming in the pit of her stomach. "They did it. They actually left us here." Unspoken was the other obvious conclusion. They were matchmaking. After witnessing a lifetime of verbal combat and zealous competition, those two hopeless romantics actually thought there was some capacity for them to kiss and make up. More like kiss and "make out," she thought with a flutter in her stomach.

She closed her eyes and fought the urge to throw up.

"They left us here," she repeated inanely, almost as if saying it aloud would make it not so.

"You're a real quick study, Brannigan," Clay grumbled,

then added under his breath, "Expectant father or not, when I get my hands on my brother, I'm going to rearrange his face but good."

Still stunned by what they'd done, and by the prospect of spending seven days and nights alone with Clay, Maddie balled up the paper in her hand. Damn them! Damn their well-intentioned, matchmaking hides.

"You can have a go at it after I get through with him," she sputtered, then turned on her heel and headed for the cabin, making a decision on the spot.

"What do you think you're doing?"

"I'm going after them."

He hooted with laughter. It was not a sound of amusement. "After them? Lady, you're screwier than I thought if you think you can find your way out of these mountains on foot. Not to mention, after your long hike, you've still got to find a way back to Jackson—and that's *if* you actually manage to locate the road."

Driven by a stark, undefinable certainty that she could survive the elements before she could survive a week in Clay James's presence, she trotted determinedly up the porch steps and jerked open the door. "I don't have to find my way back to Jackson. I only have to catch up with Emma and Garrett. They can't have gotten that far."

Besides, she told herself, she'd found her way back to the cabin just now, hadn't she? Maybe her instincts weren't as bad as she'd thought. And right now every instinct she owned was screaming at her to get as far away from this man as fast as her size sixes would take her.

"If you think they're just idling their way over the mountain, forget it. From the looks of those hoof prints, they're making fast tracks to make sure we don't try to trail them. Besides, you couldn't find your way out of a paper bag, let alone pick up Garrett's trail when he's of a mind to hide it."

"Thanks so much for the vote of confidence," she flung over her shoulder as the screen door slammed behind her, "but I think I can handle it."

Taking the loft stairs two at a time, she flew to her duffel bag, found her walking shoes and plunked down on the bed. She was lacing the last shoe tight when she heard the weight of footsteps on the loft stairs.

"You're not going anywhere." Arrogant anger spiked every word.

She didn't have to look up to know that he was standing at the top of the loft stairs glaring at her—or that his scowl was as black as midnight.

"Last I knew, you didn't run my life, James." Snagging her jacket from the duffel, she shouldered past him, trotted down the stairs and back outside.

The hard slam of the screen door told her he'd barreled right after her. The harsh grip of his hand on her upper arm was her first clue that he'd caught up with her.

"I know this is a novel idea," he growled, spinning her around to face him, "but try using your head for a change. Look," he demanded, stabbing a finger toward the sky. "In about an hour it's going to be raining pitchforks and hammer handles, and the wind's going to be whipping like a blender. Like it or not, you're not going anywhere."

She raised her face to the storm brewing in the sky, then lowered it to the one brewing in his eyes. The choice was simple.

"I'll take my chances on the weather."

Then she pulled away from his grip and started hiking as fast as she could, needing as much distance between them as possible.

Behind her, she heard his crude, graphic oath. "You are really beginning to tick me off, Matilda."

"Good and mad are you, Clayton?" she retorted without turning around. "If so, then my work here is done."

She broke into a jog, headed across the valley and aimed for the trail she prayed Emma and Garrett had taken.

"Fine," he shouted, his voice reaching her from a growing distance. "Go. Go get yourself lost. I don't give a damn. If you're not any smarter than that, then you deserve whatever happens to you.

"You need a keeper, you know that?" he added, when his diatribe failed to slow her down. "Well, it's sure as hell not going to be me."

Without turning around or slowing her stride, she flipped a hand gesture over her shoulder to let him know exactly what she thought of his opinions.

"Okay. That's it," he yelled, his tone as much as his words telling her he was washing his hands of her. "You're on your own, Brannigan. Don't say I didn't warn you. And don't expect me to come looking for you to save your sorry hide. And one more thing—when you come dragging back here, wet and cold and humble, and I *will* expect humility, don't plan on me feeling sorry for you, either!"

That was the last she heard from him.

And that's the last thought she gave to going back. It was a point of honor now. She would find Emma and Garrett if it killed her. She would not give him the satisfaction of getting lost.

For all her professed reasons for making her way out of the valley, though, the one that truly propelled her was of a far more intimidating nature. No way, no chance, no how was she going to spend seven nights in a cabin with that man. Not when she despised him the way she did. Not with the way he managed to anger her and humiliate her and...and...and make her melt with one look from those bedroom blue eyes.

"Damn woman. Damn fool woman," Clay muttered as he glared through the rain-streaked panes of the cabin window.

For a man who was not prone to profanity, he sure seemed to be spouting his share lately. He had Maddie Brannigan to thank for that. And for this roiling in his gut every time he thought of her out there alone in the mountains in this storm.

He checked his watch, raked his hands through his hair. Two hours. It had been two hours since he'd watched that trim little butt bounce off into the sunset and out of sight.

"The stubborn little fool," he uttered under his breath as guilt and worry battled for top billing.

It would be dark in another fifteen or twenty minutes. She should have been back by now. With her tail tucked between her legs. With humility oozing from every pore. With an apology for doubting his advice about the storm and defying his orders to stay put.

Yeah, right. Fat chance she'd come back. He'd seen to that. He'd goaded her and dared her and for good measure he'd made sure she knew he thought she didn't have a raindrop's chance in a forest fire of finding Garrett and Emma. Maddie come back? There was no way her sassy, stubborn pride would allow her to turn around and face his barrage of *I told you so*s.

He swore again. There was a fool on the mountain all right. But it was him, not her. And she might be in big trouble because of it.

He couldn't stand it any longer. Snagging his jacket from the rack by the door, he shrugged into it. Slamming his Stetson tight and low, he barreled out into the wind and rain....

She may be stubborn, and she may be as infuriating as sandpaper on a blister, but he couldn't leave her out there in this weather and to her own pitifully inadequate devices any longer.

As he ducked his head and set off at a jog across the

valley, he told himself he was going to take supreme, un-
mitigated pleasure in spanking her like a recalcitrant five-
year-old when he got his hands on her.

If he got his hands on her.

That thought above all others weighed on him like a
boulder. He didn't want her hurt. For all the grief she gave
him, for all the guff he put up with, the thought of a mild,
uncomplicated life without her there to mess it up was
oddly, uncomfortably unappealing.

With a renewed sense of urgency and an unreasonable
curl of anxiety clutching at his chest, he picked up the pace.
Then, for the first of what would be too many times before
this night was finally over, he called out her name.

Five

Maddie came to her senses slowly. The pain was quick to follow. It was sharp and stark and as acute as the lightning strike that sliced the sky in jagged halves. As demanding as the thunder that dogged its heels and rumbled through the mountains like the roar of a runaway train.

In the next moment came silence. With it was an instinctive awareness that she was in danger of the highest degree.

She was down, clinging to moss-covered rock. Her right arm was hooked over something...a branch or a tree root, she realized at the same time she remembered the fall.

"Oh, God," she whispered to a night grown black and the hard driving rain, and prayed she wasn't in as much trouble as it seemed.

Some prayers, she'd learned long ago, went unanswered. She accepted that this was destined to be one of them when she realized that the ground on which she lay was a precariously narrow ledge jutting from the side of the mountain.

A scream of sheer terror welled up in her throat. She fought it down along with a helpless, clawing panic and made herself assess the situation.

Above her was a good twelve feet of sheer, vertical rock wall. Below her was a good twelve-hundred-foot drop, and she was sprawled on a tiny ledge.

"Stay calm," she ordered through lips numbed by rain and cold. "For Pete's sake, stay calm."

But the breath she drew to steady herself lanced pain through her left side and broke to splinters the fragile framework of her pact to settle herself down.

It all came back to her then. She'd fallen, all right. She'd done exactly what Clay had predicted she'd do. She'd gotten lost. Then she'd panicked, and after hours of wandering around in the rain trying to get her bearings, she'd slipped and tumbled head over haunches down the steep path.

The rocks, she remembered well. So did her right knee. When she tried to bend it, pain stabbed behind her kneecap, another violation to the calm that was quickly slipping further away from her grasp.

Battling a terror filled with both what she did know and what she didn't, she shifted her weight for better purchase. Exquisite pain reminded her that her right hip had connected with something good and hard, as well. When it eased, the exact moment just before she'd run out of trail came back as clear and detailed as etched glass.

In her mind she heard the serrated sound of her own scream, relived the runaway fall off the side of the mountain. Her stomach roiled at the vivid memory and then at reality as she looked up and above her into the steep, rain-slicked side of the cliff face.

She clung tighter to the tree root and refused to let herself think about what would happen if either she or it let go.

Thunder rumbled, ricocheting like kettle drums off the rock canyon walls.

Rain pelted her in the face, blurring her vision and sending a chill bone deep.

And terror, creeping, cloying, vicious in its magnitude, demanded that she let it take control.

Clay was wet to the skin. As grouchy as a grizzly. And scared out of his mind.

Where the hell was she? Each step higher into the mountain led him farther away from the cabin and her farther away from safety. Though he wasn't more than a mile from where he'd started, he'd been searching for over three hours, tracking where he could, going on blind hunches when he couldn't.

"Maddie!" For what seemed like the hundredth time he forced her name against the screaming wind. Listened. Waited. Swore when she didn't respond.

And then he heard it. A drifting sound. A far-away whimper that filtered out of the storm like a kitten mewling in the dark.

"Maddie!" he roared above the crack of thunder and the relentless wail of violently whipping tree limbs. "Maddie! Say something! For God's sake, let me know where you are."

"Clay..."

The sound of his name came as a breath of hope on a desperately floundering wind.

He cocked his head, gauged the distance, pinpointed the direction, then sprinted like hell toward the sound.

"Clay...I'm...down here."

Relief and a gut-twisting fear rumbled along his nerve endings like twin engines, building speed, storing steam as he followed the sound of her voice to the precarious edge of a killer drop-off.

His heart slamming against his ribs, he dropped to all

fours. Wiping the rain from his face, he peered over the edge.

"Sweet Jesus," he murmured when he spotted her. It was as much a prayer of gratitude as a plea for help. She looked so small, so battered and so impossibly far from his grasp.

For an interminable moment a sickening sense of helplessness paralyzed him. She was dangerously close to being lost to the mountain. A moment was as long as the sensation lasted, before the innate qualities that made him a man and made him a James took over and he got down to the business of saving her life.

When he had her safe—only when he had her safe—would he let himself sort out this dark need that gripped him, a need that was tightly interwoven with fear and crowded with another emotion so intense he didn't know how to define it.

"Hey, hotshot," he said, borrowing from a miserly store of calm to defuse the panic they were both feeling. "Hang around this spot often?"

Bless her, she accepted the gesture for what it was and in a withering voice that she tried valiantly to keep from breaking, managed to say, "Actually n-no. Th-this is the f-first t-time I've d-dropped by."

Her voice was weak, but not her spirit. It was her spirit he needed to pull her through this.

"Kind of a dive," he said, whipping off his Stetson as he calculated the exact distance and the danger. He shrugged hurriedly out of his jacket. "How about we blow this pop stand and find someplace with a little less atmosphere?"

Her unsteady, "Fine by me," was long in coming. The tears in her voice were so thick he felt them like a punch in his gut. Urgency worked hard to undercut his own bid for control.

"Are you hurt?" he asked, all business suddenly as he prepared for the worst and prayed for better.

"Some. A little," she admitted and this time he heard the pain as well as the panic.

"Will you be able to help me when I reach you?"

More silence then a determined, "Yes."

"Good girl. How much maneuvering room have you got down there?"

"I...I don't know. Not much. This ledge...it's maybe a yard wide...less deep. It's...it's... Oh, God, Clay..." A short, unintentional, and utterly heartbreaking sound escaped her before she found her voice again. "It's c-crumbling!"

"Easy. Just go easy," he coaxed softly. "I can't have you bailing out on me now, Matilda." His prompting was gentle but firm as he hurried to wrestle off his heavy denim shirt and knot a sleeve to the sleeve of his jacket. "Just hang in and hang on and I'll get you out of there in no time. Now, can you get up on your knees?"

In answer, he heard the catch of her breath, then the catch of his own above the din of the storm—all to the ominous, ringing echo of falling stone.

"It's letting loose. Clay...please. Get me out of here!"

"I will, sweetheart. I will, just hang on and look above you." Slowly he lowered the makeshift denim rope over the edge. "Do you see my jacket?"

"Y-yes."

"Can you reach it?"

In answer, he felt the slight pressure as she grabbed and hung tight. The relief that rolled through him was tempered by anxiety. They still had a long way to go.

"Atta girl. How good a hold can you get on it?"

"I...not good."

"Can you use it for leverage to help you stand?"

Another protracted silence, this one wrought with her

fear and indecision was magnified by the sounds of the storm.

Again he prompted her with gentle firmness. "The ledge will hold, Maddie. Trust it and trust me. Just stick close in. Use the jacket and anything else you can latch on to, to lever yourself to your feet. Once you're up, get a good grip on it, tell me when you're ready, and I'll ease you up."

The sound of her shifting and the clatter of falling rock stopped his heart.

"I can't do it!" she cried, so close to slipping over another kind of edge, he had to steel himself from climbing down and losing them both.

"You can," he ordered in a hard voice. "You will. You can do this. *We* can do this. Now get a good hold of that jacket and ease to a stand."

Later he would remember a moment of fear so quelling, so pregnant with doubt that it would nearly bring him to his knees. Now he only waited with clogged breath and clammy palms and counted on her grit to get her through.

Finally he felt the tug of her weight, heard the scramble and shift of stone beneath her feet. Then, at long last, a breathless, "I'm up."

"Good. Good going, hotshot. You doing okay?"

Her hastily uttered, "Yeah," held little conviction and less confidence. Her labored breaths, rising up and over the cliff face, were wrought with exertion and pain.

He blocked the helplessness of the sound, knowing he had to keep pressing. Her greatest test was yet to come.

"That's fine. Just fine. Now hang on and climb, and I'll do the rest."

A weak, frantic, "Oh, God," had him pinching his eyes shut.

"It'll be okay." He willed his voice to be steady, confident. "You've got strong hands, Maddie. Potter's hands.

Use them. Just hang on to the jacket and know that I'm holding on, too.''

When her only reaction was no reaction, and he was afraid she was freezing up on him, he kept up a steady, reassuring monologue. ''Did I ever tell you I aced knot tying as a Boy Scout? First one in the troop to earn that particular badge,'' he rambled on in a soothing tone, giving her precious time to gather her composure, laying the ground work for the confidence she'd need to make the climb.

''Remember that time I tied you to that old oak tree in your backyard? Took your old man and mine and a Swiss Army knife to set you free. I'm still that good, little girl. It's one thing I never forgot how to do. So, count on those knots to hold. And count on me, Maddie. Count on this ol' Boy Scout up here. Put your feet to the rock face and let me pull you on up where you can give me hell again for that stunt I pulled all those years ago.''

Silence. Paralyzing. Weighted.

''You still with me?'' he demanded, more harshly than he'd intended because her life hung in the balance of her reply.

Finally, from that twelve-foot distance that seemed as vast as the mountain to which they both clung, came a watered-down version of her fiery wit.

''You better not have l-lost your edge, James. So help me…if these knots l-let loose, I'll come back and h-haunt you.''

A smile of relief twisted grim lips. She was still with him. And she was still fighting.

''There's not gonna be any haunting around here—not on that count, but dammit, Matilda, I sure as the world wish you'd set your mind to do this sometime soon. I'm as wet as a sponge up here and I'd like to get this show on the road.''

"C-Clay."

All bravado was gone.

Everything inside him thundered to a sliding stop. He couldn't keep the rusty hitch of apprehension out of his voice. "Yeah, hotshot?"

"D-don't let go."

He swallowed hard. Drew a deep breath. "Get your little butt up here and then we'll see about letting go.

"Now," he demanded calmly, leaving no room for any answer but the one he wanted, "are you ready?"

He could almost feel her gathering her courage, as precious seconds ticked by.

"Ready."

He didn't wait so much as a heartbeat. "Okay then. Here we go. Real easy now."

Flat on his belly on the rock, the cold stone biting into his bare chest, the rain peppering his bare back, he began to gather the rope of denim.

"I'm going to reel you in like some little old catfish. Just come with me. That's it," he praised her, grunting with the effort and the angle of her ascending weight. "Slow and easy. Hang on tight and dig with your feet."

Hand over hand, steady and slow, he pulled, making himself ease her along the wall of rock instead of jerking her up with all his might the way he wanted to.

It was a brutally sluggish ascent, made difficult by the rain-slicked rock and the wet denim.

After what seemed like forever, he heard the sound of her overtaxed breathing grow nearer. After what seemed like another eternity he connected with the knotted sleeves.

"We're halfway home," he grunted. "Just a little farther now."

The prospect fueled his energy and renewed his sense of urgency. He reeled faster. After three long, hard pulls, he connected with the slender circumference of her wrist.

"Thank you, God," he whispered in the same moment she cried out, less in desperation than relief, less in fear than in belief. Her other hand groped wildly into the dark empty pocket of space. He dropped the jacket and snagged her flailing hand in his.

"I've got you," he grunted as he dragged her farther away from danger and closer to the top of the mountain.

"I've got you." He all but swore in triumph as he hauled her the last yard, up and over the cliff face.

"I've got you," he growled in sweet, glorious relief as he rolled with her wrapped in his arms away from the deadly edge and into the dripping overhang of a heavily branched pine.

"I've got you," he murmured again and again into her sodden curls as she clung and he clung and the violent trembling of her body assured them both she was safe in his arms.

It took them both several heart-thundering, breath-catching moments to truly acknowledge that she was out of harm's way. It took several more before Clay could attach a thought to the anger he should be feeling for the danger she'd placed herself in.

He was certain that he was about to lay into her with both barrels when she turned her wet, sweet body closer into his and lifted her face to the rain. And in that moment, like the night, his anger faded to black, and a dark, intense awareness took its place.

The small hands that had been clinging to his bare shoulders in desperation, did so now in a studied, sensual exploration. The dark eyes that had shone so wildly with fear now met his with a steady, unblinking yearning.

"Damn you." It was barely a breath into the night, less admonishment than concession for what was about to happen. "I ought to beat you within an inch of your life for putting yourself in such danger."

"I know." Her eyes still wide and focused, she held his gaze as the tentative touch of her fingers tracked a path along his jaw. "I know," she murmured again and coaxed his head down to hers.

Knowing full well the consequences, he let her.

It was wrong. He knew it was wrong. But it was necessary. It was vital. And it was the one thing he couldn't have stopped even if the earth did.

With a muttered oath, he covered her mouth with his. Not with the gentle caress of assurance she needed, but with the totality of the fear he'd felt for her but hadn't let himself give in to. The fear was latent but full-blown, fueled by a bruising relief that they'd beaten the mountain and the elements and the night.

She didn't shrink away from the contact that bordered on brutal. She met his kiss full measure, all energy and urgency and need. She'd cheated death. Now she celebrated life, ferociously clinging, desperately craving the strength and the heat of his body and the elation of her victory in his arms.

It all crashed in on Clay then. This need she'd incited to a full-blown riot in his blood. The anger that resurfaced at the thought she'd almost been lost.

He'd never been more angry with another human being in his life. And he'd never been so relieved. He swore through a deep, drugging kiss. She cried out and drew him closer still. And then he soothed while she whimpered. And took while she gave.

And on that cold, wet, rocky summit, with the rain battering and the wind restless and wild, something changed unalterably between them. It wasn't something they could acknowledge or even name. It only was. And it seemed destined to happen as he rolled her beneath him, dominating her as he had the mountain, setting them adrift on the wind of this new storm the two of them had created.

A loud crack of thunder had her clamoring closer in his arms and startling him back to harsh, cold reality. Even now, as he held her huddled against him, he felt the trembling she tried and failed to stem. She may be safe from the cliff face, but she wasn't out of danger. He had to get her out of the storm before she went into shock.

He pressed her cheek against his bare chest. "We've got to move out, Maddie. I've got to get you out of this weather."

If possible, she snuggled closer. Then, reluctantly, she finally allowed enough room between them so that he could stand and give her a hand up. He snagged his sodden hat then watched on as she gingerly rose and eased her weight onto her right leg.

"You're hurt."

"No," she insisted, even as she grimaced through what clearly was pain.

"You're hurt," he repeated gruffly, daring her to deny it again.

She shook her head, dragged a heavy fall of wet curls away from her face. "It's just a bruise. I'll work it out."

She worked it out all of two heavily limping steps before he swung her into his arms and began the slippery descent back to the valley.

A long hour later Clay climbed the cabin steps. With a labored breath he closed the cabin door behind them with a solid kick and shut the storm outside. Maddie was shaking violently now—whether from shock or cold or a deadly combination of both he didn't know. He knew of only one way to make it stop. He had to get her warm and he had to do it fast.

Flipping on the light in the great room with his elbow, he carried her directly to the bathroom. In clench-jawed silence and ignoring any thoughts of decorum, he stripped

her, then reached past her to turn on the shower. Then he
tugged off his own clothes and led her with him into the
warm fingers of the shower spray.

Steeling himself against the feel of her wet, quivering
body against his, he held her until the worst of her trembling finally subsided. Then he gently bathed her and
washed her hair.

All the while she watched him in silence, her dark eyes
misty and trusting and devoid of fear. With tenderness and
skill, and a dogged determination to see to her injuries and
nothing else, he cleansed the jagged scratch that ran diag-
onally across her temple. Assured by her response to his
gruff "How many fingers?" test and satisfied the hot water
had dispelled most of her chill, he urged her out of the
shower.

Drawing a deep breath, he assessed the angry red welt
on her ribs, just below the full curve of her breast. Then
he probed the slight swelling around the bruising at her
knee. At each touch, she flinched, but didn't cry out as the
bite of peroxide set her scraped flesh on fire.

When he was finally certain she'd come out of this with
only minor scrapes and bruises, he wrapped first her body
then her hair in a thick towel. After knotting a towel at his
own hips, he picked her up and carried her up the stairs to
the loft bedroom.

She snuggled against him like a child. A surge of pro-
tectiveness filled his chest as he eased her to her feet beside
the bed, then held her steady while he turned down the
covers.

Turning back to her, he unwrapped her towel and laid
her on the feather bed.

It wasn't until he opened his mouth to urge her to sleep
that he realized how hard he'd clenched his jaw shut.

All this time—while he'd undressed her, held her lush,
naked body flush against his in the shower, tended to her

injuries, cradled her warmth against his chest—he'd made himself think in terms of first aid and helping hands. With studied detachment, he'd distanced himself from seeing her as a woman.

All this time he'd been able to hold it together.

Or so he'd thought.

She'd been hurting. She'd had a need.

But as he laid her down, it was his own need that raged at him to let it take over, his own need that demanded to be heard.

He almost lost it then. His control. His determination not to take advantage. As she lay there, her supple body so perfect and soft, the pale flesh of her breasts and belly all rosy and glowing—and her eyes—slumberous and languid and asking for something she couldn't possibly want, he almost followed her down on that feather bed.

He'd never in his life seen her this way—silent, compliant—though he'd thought a thousand times that he'd wanted to.

And here she was, those things and more. She was vulnerable and desirable and more beautiful than any woman had a right to be. His sex reacted to the erotic picture she made. Soft sexuality. Seductive submission. He'd wanted her this way, too. A week ago he wouldn't have been able to admit it. He couldn't deny it now.

But neither could he deny that a silent Maddie was a troubling Maddie. Though he'd never admit it to her, right about now he'd give his right arm to hear some sharp, biting comment from that viper's mouth of hers. Anything to know that she was truly all right and to break this sensual spell that spun like a silken cocoon around them.

Yet when he looked at her mouth at this moment, it wasn't a shrew that he thought of. He thought of the feel of her lips beneath his on that high mountain cliff. He thought of the way she'd tasted, exotically sweet, erotically hungry. He thought of the thunder that had raged around them and the storm that had been building in his loins. And he knew it was time to get the hell out of Dodge.

She needed rest. And from him all she needed was to be left alone.

With a clenched jaw and an unsteady hand he pulled the covers to her chin, then turned away from the bed while he still had the strength to leave her.

"Don't go."

Her whispered plea was a tantalizing caress in the intimacy of the night. It tethered him where he stood, when the only right thing to do was walk away.

But temptation had never been this seductive. Need had never been this great.

Fighting both, he made himself take that step.

The rustle of bedclothes, the softness of her fingers at his wrist stopped his movements and his heartbeat.

She didn't say a word. She didn't have to.

Without turning to face her, he let out a ragged breath, shook his head. "This isn't smart, Maddie."

Her reply, when it finally came, was sunrise soft but as inevitable as nightfall. "You think I don't know that?"

When he thought he could trust himself, he turned to face her. "Then why?"

The eyes that met his were swimming with confusion and wonder and need. "I don't know." Her breath caught on a throaty little hitch. "I don't want to know. I just want...just please...don't go."

She was so fragilely beautiful lying there. So achingly seductive.

And he was only so strong.

With a final, failed attempt at telling himself he was making the mistake of his life, he leaned over her. Damp, dusty curls framed her face in a soft wild tumble as a small hand lifted to touch his face while the other reached for the towel at his waist.

"Maddie," he murmured, as he joined her in the nest of feather ticking and age-softened quilts. "Promise me you won't hate me for this later."

"There is no later," she whispered, opening her arms then arching her back on a sigh as his dark head lowered to nuzzle her breast. Her artist's hands, with their slender fingers, combed through his hair as his mouth cruised healing kisses to the welt along her ribs.

"There is no later," she repeated, guiding his mouth to hers. "Only now…only now."

And Maddie lost herself in now.

This man…oh, this man. He was steel and velvet. Tenderness and temptation. Every move he made was magic. The slow, deliberate glide of his big hands down her back. The brush of his fingers, lingering on every ridge of her backbone, the touch of his breath, warm and deliciously unsteady, whispering across the sensitive skin of her shoulder, tracking with a feathery caress along her collarbone. There he hesitated, nuzzling her with his lips, tasting her with his tongue.

A heavy sigh, a pleasured groan, and the sensual journey of lips and breath and stubbled jaw began a downward descent. She cupped his head in her palms, slowly absorbed the texture of his hair with her fingers, the damp silk of it, the weight of it, as she lowered her head and drew in the scent of it.

The glide of his hands along her back, though slow, became more than exploration, less than honest greed as he increased the kneading pressure and drew her closer.

The flow of his hands was delicious. They were calloused and rough, sensually abrasive, his strength gentled by a determined lack of urgency, electrified with a carefully banked need. And his mouth, his mouth was like liquid

fire, heated by desire, tempered by patience and by promises of pleasures to come. Promises that he delivered.

A nip to her shoulder told of his hunger. A leisurely
scrape of teeth along her arched neck pleasured them both.
A slow, licking glide of his tongue toward her breast mellowed, then excited, and introduced them both to the
sharper side of anticipation.

With delicious languor his open mouth cruised along the
inner swell of her breast. With maddening thoroughness he
tasted the essence of her, breathed heat that elicited a
shiver, tracked kisses that wrung out a moan. And then he
found her center at last, drew the tight bud of her nipple
into his mouth and feasted.

Sensation spiked through her blood like a fever, then shot
like mercury from that sensitive point of pleasure to the
deepest heart of her need, where it curled and burned, then
tugged, drawing her tight like the string of a bow.

The pleasure was acute, frighteningly so. She cried his
name, tried to pull away, but his big hands held her gently
captive as he opened his mouth wider around her breast
and drew her deeper into his mouth and deeper under his
spell.

With a breathy moan she gave in, gave up the fight and
let the sensations flow. Like a feather on a silken breeze,
she drifted, rode the delicious thermal currents of his lovemaking and let him take her wherever the winds of his
desire decided to go.

Clay had never tasted such sweetness. Never touched
skin as soft, never needed this badly. Her breathless little
sounds, her quicksilver responses fired more than desire,
but less, much less than greed. He'd always found pleasure
in lovemaking. In both the taking and the giving. But never
so much in the giving. Her restless motions thrilled him.
Her needful, uninhibited touches arrested him.

And when he finally cupped the heat of her, slipped his

finger into the hot liquid center of the heart of her, he thought he'd explode from the sheer erotic rush.

She was slick like honey, soft like velvet and burned as hot as his burgeoning need. He pleasured her with an elicit touch and a slow steady rhythm that had her writhing against his fingers with a hunger and a desperation bred of the urgency he'd incited.

He stirred her deep and her heartbeat quickened. Deeper still and she came apart for him. He covered her cry with his mouth and her body with his and guided himself deep inside.

Then all he felt was sensation. The sweet, tight clenching of her body, the languorous drift of her hands down the length of his back, the steady regrowth of her desire as she arched her hips to his and rode with him toward yet another stunning, unparalleled peak.

He wanted to savor her. He wanted to saturate his senses with her essence and stretch this exquisite side of pleasure that he'd glimpsed with other women but never fully known. But the feel of her beneath him, holding him, taking all of him, transitioned from what he wanted to what simply had to be.

He had to be deeper.

He had to be a part of her.

And he had to believe, as he careened over that desperate edge where instinct ruled and rational thought ceased, that what he was with her, right now, was all he would ever need to be.

Six

Maddie woke up alone—alone and devastatingly conscious of what had happened last night. Not just her scrape with death, but her night with Clay in this bed.

She rolled to her back, aware of a gray morning and a light mist of rain frosting the loft windows. The slight movement made her aware of other things, as well: the stiffness in her limbs and the bruises from her fall; the sensitivity of her slightly swollen breasts...the lingering tenderness caused by the presence of man between her thighs.

She closed her eyes on a sensual sigh. Not just any man. A little shiver of excitement eddied through her. He was a sensitive man, a needy man, loving and giving and voracious and vital.

What she and Clay had shared last night had been beautiful. And wonderful. And incredible. And a hundred other things she couldn't put to words.

And now, apparently, she decided, fighting an unexpected ache of loss as she drew her conclusions from his absence, it was also over.

Well, what did she expect? It wasn't as if there was any love lost between them. It wasn't as if they liked each other or anything. Anything like love.

She closed her eyes, drew a deep breath. *Talk about sleeping with the enemy.*

Battling another unwarranted sting of disappointment, she cursed that part of her that had conjured up notions of love and romance and knights in shining armor. She cursed her sentimental heart.

"Face it, Matilda," she told herself pragmatically. "What you shared last night had nothing to do with romance. It had everything to do with shock and fear and adrenaline. And sex. It had a lot to do with sex. Don't confuse the issue."

But for some reason, she *was* confused. Very confused, because it had felt like so much more.

"So," she wondered aloud, sifting through her muddled thoughts, "where do you go from here?"

If you're Clay James, evidently you exit stage left. Given their history, it shouldn't have come as a surprise that he'd bailed. It shouldn't have hurt, either. But again, for some reason, it did. It hurt even more than her knee when she forced herself to bend it. More than her head that pounded in complaint when she sat up on the edge of the bed.

Gathering her hair away from her face with one hand, and the sheet to her breasts with the other, she looked around the loft bedroom. To the unknowing eye, it appeared as pristine and celibate as it had after every other night she'd spent here while Emma and Sara Jane had slept in the bedroom downstairs.

Only it wasn't pristine. Not anymore. And last night had ended what many would be surprised to learn was several years of celibacy for her. But, oh, what an end, she thought as she limped to her duffel and rummaged around for panties, a pair of old jeans and an oversize kelly green sweater.

End, she concluded, as she struggled into her clothes then dragged a brush through her hair, seemed to be the key word here.

End. She mulled the word around in her mind. It had to be one of the most efficient words in the English language. Concise. Severing. Final.

Well, that was fine. And it was definitely for the best. "I mean, really. Maddie Brannigan and Clay James together...as a couple?" she mused aloud, hoping that hearing the words would imprint on her mind how ridiculous the notion was. "It wasn't only laughable, it was ludicrous."

Committed to that conclusion, she faced the loft stairs and prepared herself to face the music. It took as much strength of will as it did physical stamina, but she gathered both and hobbled barefoot down the steps to confirm what she'd already guessed. Not only had Clay left her bed, he'd left the cabin. He wasn't far, she was sure, but far enough to drive home his point. He was sorry about what had happened between them. Well, so was she. Sort of. Not as much as she should be.

His obvious regret stung, though. She hadn't been prepared for the bite.

"Well, you should have been," she muttered as she limped to the kitchen. He hadn't bargained for last night. He'd made it clear, in fact, what a bad idea he thought it was.

Boy, had he been right. This was a mess.

"You made the deal," she reminded herself unnecessarily as she filled a mug with coffee from a pot that appeared to have been brewed hours earlier. "You're the one who said, There is no later."

Only there was. And it was here. And so far, it wasn't much fun.

Leaning back against the counter, she wrapped her hands around the warm mug and tried to figure out how she was going to face him. It was the classic uncomfortable morning after. Only it was worse because they didn't have just one morning to muddle through, but several more to weather.

She hadn't gotten past how to deal with this first one when she heard the cabin door creak open, then close.

She'd known meeting his eyes wouldn't be easy. It turned out that it was worse than hard. That was because some small part of her—the eternal, sappy optimist, probably—had been holding out a tiny pocket of hope. She wasn't sure why, but she'd been hoping she was wrong. Hoping that his disappearing act didn't mean what his eyes assured her it did.

No morning-after lover's smile tilted his lips or softened his eyes. No words like "Last night was wonderful, let's go see if we can make magic together again," tumbled from his sensual lips—lips that had cruised over her body with such intimate attention to her needs.

The memory of his mouth and his hands and his body poised over hers sent an arc of arousal sizzling through her blood, a wave of longing that weakened her knees and stalled her breath.

It was those touches, those memories that were confusing her. She'd seen a side of Clay last night she'd never seen before. A tender, giving side that had been as sensual as it was surprising. As welcome as it was refreshing.

All that was gone now. The look in his eyes—cautious, assessing, wary—brought her back to the moment like an ice-water shower. Reality was staring her in the face: this was no willing lover wanting to take her back to bed.

This wasn't even a friend. This was a man truly and

totally at a loss as to how to handle the morning-after regrets of a mistake of epic proportions.

"How are you?" he asked gruffly, still rooted like an
oak tree just inside the door. His hand went up stiffly, a
vague gesture meant to encompass her entire body. "How's
the knee? And your head? There are aspirin in the bathroom
if you need them."

She held his gaze for only a moment, wondering why
she was searching for a sign that he was concerned about
more than just a physical inventory of the state of various
injuries to her body. But there was nothing more than a
clearly self-conscious effort on his part to act concerned,
seem concerned.

Coward. Why don't you ask me about my heart, she
thought miserably. *Ask me if it's aching. Ask me about my
pride. It's not in the best shape, either.*

She nipped those thoughts at the bud stage. There was
nothing wrong with her heart. It had no investment here.
Her pride, maybe, but not her heart.

Shape up, she ordered herself mentally. You're both
grown-ups here. This isn't the first time two consenting
adults who had absolutely nothing in common had found
common ground in the dark of night in each other's arms.

Chalking up her melodramatic musings to a little leftover
shock, she lifted her chin and met his scowl. "My knee's
fine," she assured him.

"And the head?" he persisted, walking toward her.

She couldn't help it. When he drew near, she flinched
and moved away. He stopped, his big hand poised midair
before he reached past her to snag the coffeepot and fill his
mug.

She ducked her head and bashed herself for worsening
what was already a difficult situation. He'd only wanted
coffee. He hadn't been reaching for her—out of affection
or pity or any other emotion.

She forced a shaky breath. "Fine. The head is fine," she said with a smile that convinced neither of them that she was as relaxed about this mess as she pretended to be.

Thankfully he didn't press, and she didn't offer more information. Instead, they both stared uncomfortably at anything and everything but each other.

Silence settled. Strung with tension. Crowded with unease. Through it she could hear the soft sound of his breathing, the rustle of his chambray shirt against his skin, and outside, the whisper of the wind through the pines. Above it she could hear the rumble of his regrets and the sound of her pride shattering. Beneath it all she could hear the roar of the mistake she had made.

And it *had* been *her* mistake. She'd done the asking. She'd extended the invitation, then made sure he couldn't refuse it. That meant it was up to her to fix it—and to hopefully salvage some self-respect in the process.

She'd let him see her vulnerability only once before. She'd promised herself then that she'd never let it happen again. If she didn't want to crumble like a week-old cookie, she was going to have to pull herself together. Fast.

"Look," she said, all false bravado and blind determination, "about last night."

"Maddie," he began, the promise of an apology heavy in his tone.

"No, wait." She hurriedly cut him off, stalling whatever guilt-ridden words he was about to say. She couldn't stand hearing them. Not yet. Maybe not ever. "I need to say this, Clay. And you need to hear it."

When he conceded with a scowl and a reluctant nod, she drew a deep breath and began again. But not before she walked away from the counter and several feet away from him. Distance was imperative if she was going to get through this.

"Here's the deal," she said, looking from her coffee

mug to the view of the mist-shrouded valley outside the window. "I had a need last night. Evidently, so did you. We...we were both caught up in a huge adrenaline rush, maybe even a little too much firsthand knowledge of how precarious life really is. Of how one moment could potentially be the last. And of how fragile we are as a human race."

"Fragile," he repeated as she finally mustered the courage to face him. His mouth was grim, his dark brows drawn low over the unnatural calm of his eyes. "Human race."

"Yes," she said, ignoring the fact that she felt about as convinced as he looked. "It was a moment, Clay. One that I promised myself I wouldn't regret when it was over. And I don't regret it. I don't want you to, either."

He hadn't moved. His expression hadn't changed. He looked like a thundercloud about ready to let loose as that tell-all muscle began to twitch above his right eye.

"Just what am I supposed to feel—if you don't mind my asking."

Her gaze skittered from his to her hands, which were still clutching the coffee mug in a death grip. *What is he supposed to feel?* Something. Something for me, maybe, she thought morosely, knowing by the hard look on his face that the possibility of *that* happening was negligible to nonexistent. And knowing that they still weren't friends. Last night hadn't changed that situation.

"Well, for starters, as I said, no regrets." She was determined not to let him see the pain she was at a loss to explain away or understand. "And for heaven's sake, no guilt."

Statues should stand so still. "And that's it. No regrets. No guilt."

This wasn't going exactly how she'd thought it would. He was supposed to look relieved. What he looked was royally ticked off.

"We-e-ll." She drew the word out and tried again, grop-ing for the key to his reactions. "I...I guess we could both feel fortunate that...that it was a pleasurable experience," she suggested a little uneasily.

"Pleasurable?"

He looked like he'd like to chew nails, spit them out and pin her to the wall with them.

"Yes," she said warily. "It...it was pleasurable. Any-way, it was for me...that is, what I remember of it was."

Nuclear warheads presented less threat than the look on his face. "What you *remember?*"

Now she'd done it. His reaction—confusing as it was—had rattled her so much that she'd taken the coward's way out. She'd resorted to the old "I don't remember every-thing" ploy. Lame. Totally lame, but now that she'd chosen that road, she wasn't about to make a U-turn.

"Well, after all, I was a bit...traumatized. I mean, I...I'd had quite a scare. And I was exhausted. I guess I just, well, don't get me wrong, I remember making—" she stumbled over the words but made herself continue "—making love with you," she managed softly and prayed to God she didn't embarrass herself more by blushing, "but...but a lot of details are...are kind of fuzzy."

His jaw clenched to granite. "Fuzzy?"

She wished he'd quit repeating everything she said, like the words left a foul taste in his mouth and he had to spit them out or gag on them.

"Well, yes. I mean, it...ah, it...well, it wasn't exactly—I mean, *I*," she clarified when the blue-gray of his eyes turned to a cobalt hue that reminded her of gunmetal or a sunset storm. "*I* wasn't exactly—"

"Stop." He set his mug on the counter with a thud, held a hand in the air like a traffic cop. "I get the picture. You weren't at your best. Last night wasn't the best. And now what is best is that we just forget it ever happened. Does that about sum it up?''

When she just stood there, stung by the anger in his voice and his dark glare, he answered for her.

''Fine. That works just fine for me.'' With a final, probing look, he shoved away from the counter and stalked out the door.

Clay got as far as the bottom porch step before he stopped. For a long, riotous moment, he considered marching right back in there, hauling that mule-headed woman into his arms and kissing that crushable mouth of hers closed. She couldn't talk about guilt and regret and the human race and *pleasurable* experiences then, by God. Or about not remembering everything.

Well, he remembered. His memory was just fine, thank you very much.

Damn her. *Damn her.* But wasn't it just like her to tick him off when what he'd wanted this morning was another...hell. It didn't matter now what he'd wanted. Just like it didn't matter that he'd wanted to wake up beside her this morning, but had decided she might need a little space to herself to sort things out.

She needed space all right. Right about now so did he. A couple thousand miles ought to do it, but he'd have to settle for the woodshed. It was back to business as usual between them. Like last night had never happened. Like it never meant anything.

Evidently to her it hadn't. Well, it hadn't meant anything to him, either, he assured himself, ignoring the ache in his gut that tried to tell him otherwise.

'' 'Fuzzy,' '' he muttered as he stalked to the wood pile and snagged the ax. '' 'Didn't exactly remember.' '' Iron hit wood with a bone-jarring *thwack*. What a bunch of bull.

She remembered. She couldn't have come apart for him the way she had and then not remember.

As least, he wanted like hell to believe that was true.

Because he remembered.

Everything.

Every shivery little sigh. Every pulse-altering moan. The silk of her skin, the heat of her body, the taste of her lips. Most specifically, he remembered the moment he'd decided that they may have wasted the better part of their adult lives fighting, when they could have been making love.

Sweet love. Complete love. He closed his eyes and swallowed hard. Love as emotionally right as it was physically unparalleled.

Or so he'd thought last night.

Thwack!

Well, it was a stupid thought. And not worth the time it took to form it.

Maddie Brannigan was still the same smart-mouthed, independent little shrew she'd been all her life. They still had nothing in common. Nothing going for them but chemistry, biology, and as she'd so baldly pointed out, a mutual need.

She'd made her position on that as clear as a mountain stream. Last night had been a convenience for her. A necessary outlet for pent-up fear and, oh, yeah, an adrenaline rush.

Well, that's all it had meant to him, too. And he was going to stay out here until he was as clear on that fact as she was.

Maddie sneaked a peek out the cabin window and looked for a sign of Clay through the light drizzle. She didn't quite understand his anger. And he'd most definitely been angry.

She'd thought he would have been relieved that she was letting him off the hook—there was no way she could be wrong about that. What was wrong, she decided, as she heard the steady thwack of his ax splitting firewood, was how she'd handled it.

If she'd had it in her to feel pity for anyone but herself right now, she'd probably have felt sorry for him. She'd bruised his ego. It wasn't the escape she was offering that was giving him trouble. It was the idea that she'd implied that his lovemaking wasn't memorable enough for her to…well, to remember.

Well, shoot. It was tough to give a guy an out when your heart, for no good reason, was making noises about breaking—which of course, it wasn't. Not even close.

She pressed her forehead against the cool windowpane. She couldn't afford to let him know just how well she remembered last night. In fact, it had been the most memorable night of her life.

He'd touched her with his tenderness, moved her with his ardor, nearly destroyed her with his dedication to giving her pleasure.

Every caress, every brush of his lips to her skin was etched like golden engravings in her mind. Even as she'd stood there this morning, facing him for the first time, denying how special last night had been, every erogenous zone in her body had yearned for his touch…to tantalize, to liquefy, to electrify.

But it was more, even more than that. She hadn't realized how badly her heart hungered for the love she thought she'd seen in his eyes and felt with every stroke of his body into hers. Hadn't realized her soul had cried out for the mate she'd foolishly believed had been right underneath her nose all these years.

Stupid. Stupid. Stupid.

Love. Soul mate. Ha. Double ha.

Catering to her bruised pride and her sore knee, she made her way slowly to the bathroom. When she caught a glimpse of herself in the mirror, she groaned and considered a mercy killing—her own.

Her temple was red and purple with bruises, her face was a mass of tiny scratches and her eyes were rimmed with dark circles. Then there was her hair. It looked like she'd styled it with the help of direct current from an electrical outlet.

She braced her palms on the ledge of the sink and hung her head. The laugh, when it came, was tinged with a touch of hysteria and a demeaning dose of tears.

"Well," she told her sorry reflection, as she sucked in a rallying breath and resolved to see herself through this without losing any more of her dignity, "faced with the prospect of waking up to this every morning, can you really blame any guy for running out on you?

"No," she answered herself realistically. "You can't blame a guy at all."

Neither was she going to blame herself for what had happened, she decided as she turned on the cold water, splashed her face liberally and tried to undo some of the damage. She wasn't going to blame herself for indulging in a need that had felt righteous and wondrous and new.

She was going to be sorry, though.

She suspected that for the rest of her life she was going to be sorry that what she'd found in that man's arms had promised so much and meant so little.

The drizzle continued all day, then finally accelerated to a steady downpour by sundown. Clay had split wood until he'd raised blisters. Then he'd stacked it, restacked it and stacked it again. He'd fiddled with the water line and the pump. He'd messed with the gas-powered generator. In the process, he'd gotten soaked to the skin and managed to upgrade his mood from foul to rotten to black.

By the time he finally gave it up and climbed the steps

to the cabin, it was dark. He was cranky. He was tired. And he was hungry.

The first thing he saw when he closed the door behind him only served to sharpen the serrated blade of his temper.

Maddie, looking soft and cuddly and sexy was curled up asleep on the sofa in front of a roaring fire. The sight of her, all misty and mellow and sleep mussed, made him want to howl like a raging beast, because he didn't have the right to join her there. Because he didn't have the right to wake her with a soft kiss on her brow, brush that wild tangle of sand-gold curls away from her face and tell her with his touch how glad he was to see her.

So much for getting his head on straight.

Could you believe it? Twenty-four hours ago he could have cheerfully and without remorse turned his back on that sassy little wildcat and not given two good licks if he ever saw her or heard from her again.

Twenty-four hours ago.

Before he'd almost lost her.

Before he'd made love to her.

Before he'd held her in the night, absorbed her silky heat with his body, felt her stir and stretch and curl into him with a trust reserved for lovers.

Now he didn't know what he felt. Except the anger. He had a darn good handle on that. What he didn't have a handle on was why—even though he'd had the better part of the day to think about it.

She'd been right, of course. She'd reduced what had happened between them to exactly what it was. It was just need. Just biological, chemical need. Just sex. Hadn't he always had a curiosity about what it would be like to make love with her? Well, now that curiosity was satisfied.

Only he still didn't feel satisfied. What he felt was edgy. Among other things. Things he didn't want to think about. Things that had been giving him trouble all day.

He shrugged out of his wet jacket and hung it over the back of a chair to dry, thinking all along that he should have known. He wasn't sure what, but he just knew he should have known something, and it ticked him off even more that he couldn't put a finger on what it was.

It was like he'd forgotten everything he knew about her and their lifelong relationship. Like the fact that, except for last night in bed, the two of them mixed about as well as chili powder and chocolate sauce. Like the fact that they'd been sworn enemies since birth, he reminded himself, building on his arguments as he stalked to the kitchen sink to wash his hands. That, sure as the world, hadn't changed. She'd been a knot in his shoelace, a sliver in his finger, gum in his hair right up to the moment he'd dragged her off that cliff.

But something had changed between them then.

He could have sworn something had changed. If not then, then it had definitely changed last night.

Or so he'd thought.

Well, she'd straightened him out this morning. No regrets. No guilt. That's what she'd said. And no invitation to stick around.

Fine. More than fine. It was just dandy with him. As far as he was concerned, last night had never happened.

Now if he could just convince his body of that fact.

Obviously, that was going to be a tough trick, given the way he responded physically when she stirred and stretched like a sinuous cat, then rose from her little nest and spotted him standing there.

"Oh." The word was more sighed than spoken. "I didn't hear you come in."

He leaned his hips back against the counter and crossed his arms over his chest. "Have a nice nap?" he asked and told himself he was just being civil. He really didn't give a horse's hind end how her nap was. And he wasn't a bit relieved to see the smudges under her eyes had lightened to a soft violet, or that the bruise at her temple appeared to have lost some of its angry color. He didn't care at all.

She shot him a tight, nervous smile. "I must have slept most of the day away. But I did stay awake long enough to make us some beef stew."

"You shouldn't have—" He cut himself off when he realized he was about to say that she shouldn't have stressed herself that way when she needed to rest and recover. "You shouldn't have bothered," he amended. "I could have done fine with a sandwich."

"Well, I couldn't. I was starving. I'll heat some up if you like."

Yeah. Like, that's all he needed.

"I can get it myself," he growled, and hoped the edge in his voice sounded dismissive instead of disappointed.

Because his mother had raised a gentleman, he told himself, he offered to heat some for her, too.

"Only if you let me set the table," she said.

More domestic bliss. How nice. "Whatever."

Her gaze skittered to his, narrowed and wary. But she didn't comment. And neither did he.

They played cat and mouse through the stew. Each eating in a silence broken only by the click of a spoon to a bowl, the rustle of plastic-wrapped crackers, the scrape of a chair on the floor.

"Leave them," he ordered a little too forcefully when she reached for his dirty dishes. There was no way he was going to let her pick up after him. "I'll take care of it."

For whatever reason, she chose not to argue. She rose from the table—but not before she gave him a long, searching look—then, with a soft shrug, walked back to the sofa and the fire.

She was still limping, he noticed with more than a twinge

of concern. After rinsing the dishes in the sink, he dug out the first aid kit again.

"I'd better have another look at that knee," he said, as no-nonsense as he could manage.

She eyed him with that soft scowl that told him she was thinking about putting up a fuss. In the end she relented without a word. She did, however, hedge when it became apparent the leg of her jeans was too tight to pull up over her knee.

He let out an impatient breath and told himself he could do this. "It's a little late for decorum, don't you think? Just drop 'em and let's get this over with."

When she still hesitated, he added one more zinger. "It's not like I haven't seen it all before."

For a brief moment her eyes glassed over with moisture. And in that moment he felt an ugly blast of satisfaction for hitting a nerve. In the next he hated himself for his intentional attempt to humiliate her.

Evidently his shot hit its mark.

"Go to hell, James."

Her voice trembled with fury and the threat of tears. But her steps were purposeful and proud as she limped out of the room and up the loft stairs.

He stared at the floor, closed his eyes, uttered an oath under his breath. But he didn't apologize, and he didn't go after her.

He did admit—grudgingly—that he'd lashed out at her because he'd wanted to hurt her. He still wasn't sure why.

Dammit, he hated this. Hated the strained way things were between them. It had been easier—much easier—when they'd gone at each other without gloves, baiting and inciting and inviting fights at every turn. At least then he'd known where he'd stood with her. At least then he'd known the rules. And the rules had never been designed to intentionally hurt each other.

But last night had changed the rules. And nothing, it seemed, would ever be the same between them again.

Seven

"**W**hy did you do it?"

Maddie glanced up from her game of solitaire, startled out of her concentration by the sound of Clay's voice.

She was perched on the edge of the sofa, using a low coffee table of rustic pine for her game board. It was late afternoon of the third day. The last words they'd exchanged had been last night when she'd suggested that he take a fast trip to someplace a whole lot hotter than Wyoming in September.

To say that the night had been long was like saying the Tetons were just mountains. To say that this day had been strained was like saying the Mississippi was just a river. She saw relief from neither in sight.

All day long she'd made it a point to stay out of Clay's way. He'd made it his mission to see that she did. No mean feat for either of them with the rain confining them to the cabin.

Not that the cabin was small. It wasn't. Jonathan James had built the mountain retreat thirty years ago out of honeyed pine and rough-hewn timbers and beams, with his family in mind. The great room was mostly living area with a kitchen and dining room at one end. There was a small bathroom, the loft bedroom, and a large dormitory-style bedroom toward the rear of the structure. It was sturdy, homey and masculine. Whether looking through the windows or standing on the wrap-around front porch, it afforded a breathtaking view of the mountain range that towered over the valley and the meandering flow of glimmering silk that was Wind River.

The cabin provided everything a mountain retreat was supposed to provide. What it didn't offer was privacy. They were sequestered like jurors in the grips of a long, ugly trial.

And now he'd spoken, interloping on that small island of solitude she'd carved out of silence and a determination to shut everything else out until Garrett came to get them four long days and nights from now.

She looked up, holding loosely in her hand the deck of cards she'd found in a kitchen drawer. "I'm sorry. Did you say something?"

His blue eyes were hard—even from across the room she could see that. He'd been prowling around the cabin most of the day, tinkering with cabinet hinges and loose screws, planing a sticky door. In actuality, he'd been brooding, to her way of thinking.

For a moment he seemed to consider whether it was worth his effort to repeat the question. Finally he rolled his broad shoulders, hooked his thumbs on the front pockets of his jeans and leaned his hips against the windowsill. "Why did you do it? Why did you run?"

She went blank for a moment. Would have given him a

shrug for an answer if the look in his eyes hadn't been so intent.

Why did she run? She played the queen of hearts on the king of clubs, the six of spades on the seven of diamonds and tried to come up with an honest answer.

When none presented itself, she went back to her game, feigning absorption with the cards. "Isn't it obvious?"

She didn't have to look at his face to know he was still scowling as he shoved away from the window and stalked across the room toward her. "If it was obvious, I wouldn't be asking. Why did you run, Maddie? Was the thought of staying here with me so awful that you'd risk your life to get away?"

When she still didn't respond, he took her silence for stubbornness. Expelling a great puff of air, he laughed without humor. "And they thought things had gotten out of hand when I dumped you in the cement. Just wait until they find out I drove you over the side of a mountain."

She gave a quick shake of her head. "You didn't drive me anywhere."

The look on his face said she'd surprised him by coming to his defense. In truth, she'd surprised herself. At the moment, however, she didn't want to question her words or her motives. "I did a stupid thing. I paid the price. And unless you tell them, they don't need to know about it."

He seemed to consider that before his mouth tightened again.

Silence settled. Tentative, fretful. She used the card game as an excuse to avoid looking into his eyes. She suspected that if she did, she'd see something more than curiosity darkening them. She'd see real concern. Maybe even caring. She'd already convinced herself he was capable of neither. At least, she'd tried to.

Black jack on red queen. Four of clubs on five of hearts. Three of—

A big hand covered hers.

The warmth of his skin stopped more than her brittle, evasive motions. Her heart skidded to a halt, fluttered, then started again with a wild, reckless rhythm. In the dark of night, in the heat of passion, he'd touched her much more intimately, much more sensually, yet every erogenous zone in her body vibrated in response to the callused heat of his hand covering hers. Like his body had covered hers.

Slowly she settled herself down. Slower still, she looked up, met his eyes. There was concern there. And maybe even a little pain.

"Why?" he repeated.

Why. She'd been asking herself the same question ever since she'd realized she'd gotten herself lost up there on the mountain. What she'd done had been beyond stupid. Beyond sane. But the thought of spending a solid week with him, facing him day and night—especially the nights—had thrown her into a panic so profound, intelligence or sanity hadn't stood a chance.

She wasn't going to admit that to him, though. She couldn't confess that she'd been so afraid of giving in to her desire for him that she'd blindly run away rather than sweat it out.

Hopeless. She was hopeless and a coward and foolish to boot. And the best part was that the joke was on her. Everything she'd run away to avoid had still happened. And here she was, struggling with the insane wish that it would happen again.

When she closed her eyes and looked away, he released her hand. Swearing darkly, he dragged his fingers through his hair.

"All right, if you can't answer that, then answer this." His demand was no-nonsense and gruff. "Why do we do this to each other? Why do we bicker and snipe and constantly have to try to get the best of each other?"

Feeling very weary suddenly, she slumped back against the sofa cushions. Her admission, when it finally came, was tinged heavily with frustration, but as honest as a sunrise. "I've been wondering the same thing lately, myself."

He went utterly still, clearly surprised by her reply. Well, so was she. Any other time she'd have gladly, in typical biting form, blasted him with a laundry list of the grievances that set her off.

Since she hadn't, his features softened with the understanding that they were, at least for the moment, of the same mind on this subject. For the moment, even beyond fighting.

Uncertain how to deal with the turn of events, he reverted to one of her tactics. He feigned interest in the cards spread out on the table. "Move your black nine to the red ten," he said after a moment, then did it himself.

Momentarily stalled by his non sequitur, and his nerve, she just stared at him. When she finally recovered, her barb was knee-jerk and to the point. "Have you ever looked up *solitaire* in the dictionary?

"*Solitaire*," she began, making a show of grumbling as he sat down beside her on the sofa and she had to scoot over to make room, "means alone."

Unapologetic, he reached to make another play.

She slapped his hand.

The fool winked at her. "Just trying to help."

"So who asked for your help?" she groused, fighting the beginnings of a grin.

Completely taking over now, he neatly shifted a red seven to a black eight. "There's such a thing as double solitaire, you know."

It was the oddest thing. She hadn't actually felt the axis turn. Hadn't really sensed their world shudder and sway then ease back into its orbit. But in the last few minutes it had. As easily as a squabble over a card game, everything that was comfortable and natural and familiar between them had shifted, then settled back into place without fanfare or fuss.

They were bickering again. Like old times. Like they'd never stopped. Only the caustic edge was gone, replaced by something kinder, something gentler that made noises about being almost friendly.

He still didn't have the answers to his questions. Neither did she. For the time being, though, that was just fine. Cushioned by a teasing sort of snipe and parry, they'd settled into a comfort zone that made it easier to stay where they were than to question why it felt so right.

And, as incredible as it seemed, she understood perfectly that Clay had orchestrated the entire thing. His interference with her game had been the equivalent of offering her an olive branch. Granted, it was in the form of a prickly cactus, but it was a peace offering nonetheless.

"I don't think I need you to fill me in on double solitaire," she said, grasping it like a child reaching for ice cream. "I'm familiar with the game. I also know about gin rummy. If you want to make it worth my while, I'd be delighted to beat you at it. Repeatedly."

"Ha. You couldn't give an egg a sound beating. Deal the cards," he ordered, his dark eyes glittering with a challenge and a smile as he unbuttoned his cuffs and rolled his sleeves up to his elbows. "And prepare to eat your words. To show you what a sport I am, I'll even get the salt and pepper."

She busied herself gathering the deck and feeling relieved. "I'm beginning to remember why I don't like you, Clayton. You're too cocky for your own good."

"And I remember why I don't like you, Matilda," he said, smiling sweetly. "You're a brat. Always have been. Always will be. And a poor loser to boot."

She split the deck expertly, dovetailed the cards together,

then bridged them. "That's because I don't get that much practice at losing."

"Well, see, that's where I come in." His grin overflowed with benevolence. "I can remedy that little character flaw in no time. Deal, hotshot. And prepare to get solidly whupped."

As she dealt, she still wasn't altogether certain how they had managed to come full circle or about the subtle change in their attitudes toward each other. She only knew she didn't have this ugly, achy lump in her throat anymore. At least, it wasn't as intense as it had been. She didn't think she'd ever get over the night she'd spent in his arms, or the hurt she'd felt that it had meant so little to him. But she knew she had to get past it. He was offering her the chance. For once in her life where he was concerned, she accepted it with grace and the wisdom not to question why.

The fire had burned down to a blue-yellow glow by midnight. Clay was into Maddie for $2.76. She'd kept careful track and had his IOU tucked in her jeans pocket.

Lazy and content, they sat at either end of the sofa, their feet propped on the low pine table, an empty popcorn bowl sitting between them on the cushion.

The reminiscing had started about an hour ago. The grins had been mellow and frequent. The debates heated.

"The one that really, *really* did it," she was saying after an hour of comparing pranks and get-even schemes they'd pulled on each other over the years, "was that announcement you made over the school PA system. I thought I was going to die of humiliation. *Attention student body—*" she made a megaphone of her hands and mimicked his words *"—it has come to our attention that someone has stolen Maddie Brannigan's box of Kleenex. Whoever is responsible, please return them to her immediately so she can put the bumps back in her sweater."*

"I was inspired," he said with a lofty sigh and a self-satisfied grin.

"And I was mortified. Do you have any idea the teasing I suffered? Being fourteen and flat-chested was tough enough, yet you managed to make it unbearable."

"I did my best." Pride tinged each word. "Besides, it wasn't like you didn't have it coming."

"Oh, yeah." She snuggled deeper into the sofa, her scowl replaced by a smile of unbridled accomplishment. "I guess I did get you pretty good the week before, didn't I?"

"Pretty good?" He lowered a dark brow and glared at her. *Pretty good?*

She sighed in satisfaction for a job well done as she crossed her ankles, laced her hands over her abdomen and chuckled. "You were a sight when I got through with you."

"And all on the pretense of making nice," he sputtered, remembering how she'd invited him over to try out their new hot tub. He'd been happily soaking up the bubbles, eyes closed in decadent bliss when she'd slipped out of the tub and dumped a whole package of purple dye into the water.

"I was lavender from head to toe for a month."

"Yeah, you were. It was great. Watching you suffer through that was worth the month Mom and Dad grounded me."

"If I remember right, you missed the homecoming dance because of it."

She shrugged. "I didn't have a date, anyway. Unlike you. Rat that you were, you were busy juggling Amy Coogen, Candy Jones, and—let's see—"

"Rachael Gordon," he supplied helpfully and drummed an open hand over his chest to pantomime heartthrobs.

"Right. Good ol' Rachael. Big heart. Big chest. Big easy. Whatever happened to her, anyway?"

"After I dumped her and broke her heart, you mean?"

She snorted indelicately. "Yeah. After that."

"I think I heard that she married a gynecologist from Landers and had her fifth kid a year or so ago."

She angled a look his way. "Lots of the old gang are settled with families. Some of them on their second marriages already."

"Yeah," he said, thoughtful suddenly. He rose, opened the fire screen and eased another wedge of wood on the embers. When the flames caught hold, he settled back on the sofa and propped his feet next to hers again on the table.

For long moments they watched in a companionable silence while the fire crackled and spit. He smiled at the "Home Sweet Home" sampler hanging on the stone above the mantel. His mother had cross-stitched the sentiment when he was just a little boy.

"Why is it that you've never gotten married, Maddie?" he asked, giving her toes a gentle nudge with his. "And don't tell me it's because no one's ever been interested. I happen to know better."

Uncomfortable with the question but unaccountably pleased that he was interested, she just shrugged. "Mr. Right has yet to come aknockin'."

"And this Mr. Right, what would he be like?"

She eyed him to see if he was baiting her. Deciding he was genuinely interested, she shrugged again and gave his question some serious thought. Unsettled when she realized that all the qualities that came to mind started and ended with a description of him, she made herself do a reality check and a little hedging. "I figure I'll know him when I see him."

He shifted his hip until he was facing her, his elbow buried in the sofa back, his jaw propped in his palm. "Come on. You can do better than that. Tell me. What's a guy have to do to win Mad Dog Brannigan's heart?"

She didn't quite have it in her to bristle but she did give back as good as she got. "Well, for starters, Banana Boy—"

"That's Banana *Man*, to you," he interrupted with a grin she couldn't help but return.

"Okay, for starters, Banana Man, he'd have to be someone who doesn't call me Mad Dog."

Without remorse and without missing a beat, he pressed for more. "And for enders?"

She didn't like where this conversation was going. It was too personal. Too private and too close to her heart. "There is no such word as enders."

"We're not playing Scrabble. Just answer the question. What's important to you in a man? Money? Power? No family history of male-pattern baldness?"

"Unlike some people who will remain nameless—" she sent a meaningful glance his way "—money, power and looks aren't important to me."

He snorted. "And the sky isn't blue."

"I mean it," she insisted. "Integrity is important. And loyalty. He'd have to be someone I could trust and depend on."

"Like a Boy Scout?" he suggested gamely. "Or a basset hound?"

"Like a decent person. And he'd have to love me," she added, still surprised that it hurt a little to know that loving her was something Clay could never do. "He'd have to respect me," she went on. "Treat me like an individual and allow me to be one. In any relationship, I'd need to be my own person and be given the room to grow both emotionally and creatively."

He seemed to think about that before surprising her with yet another question. "And what would it take for a guy to completely blow you out of the water? Send you roses? Give you diamonds? A Beemer?"

He really didn't know her, she realized, and hurt a little more that he thought she was so shallow. "I'm not a roses kind of girl. Now if a guy came carrying wildflowers—ones he'd picked himself—that might score a few points. Diamonds?" She shook her head. "I'd rather have bronze or copper, sometimes maybe some gold—all for my glazes," she clarified. "Those are big expenses for my business. And as for the Beemer, I've always had this little fantasy that instead of a fancy sports car, he'd come for me on a big black horse and we'd ride off into the sunset."

And you've also got a big mouth, Brannigan. Just keep talking and you'll eventually supply him with enough ammunition to take potshots at you until you start drawing social security.

"What about you?" she asked before she got really stupid and revealed more of her secret fantasies. "You've been close to tying the knot on a couple of different occasions—Veronica the most recent case in point. Yet you never quite get the deed done. What's it going to take to finally get Clay James to the altar?"

He answered without hesitation. "Money, power and no family history of *female*-pattern baldness."

She rolled her eyes. "I'm serious. I leveled with you. Return the favor."

"Okay." He settled back again, considered. "For one thing, she'd have to be a nice person. No shrew. She'd have to be…focused…committed…attentive. To me, to our marriage. And she'd have to be content to accept me the way I am. I work hard, I play hard. I'd want her to respect that. It wouldn't hurt if she could cook, either."

All qualities, she suspected, that he felt she was sadly lacking. Oh, well. "Which leads me back to What happened with Veronica? Seems to me she fits that bill and then some."

He laced his fingers together on top of his head. "You

know," he began, then let out a deep breath and stared thoughtfully at the fire, "I'm not really sure. I thought she was the one. Only...I don't know. Something just wasn't clicking."

Like it clicked two nights ago between us? she wondered, unable to squelch the thought before it formed.

This was someplace she definitely did not want to go. She'd been fighting that memory all day. Battling it back all evening. And now it was here again. Simmering and sensual. Uncommonly vivid. And Clay, sitting beside her, smelling wonderfully of male and musk and looking as gorgeous by the wood fire as he did by daylight, didn't help one bit.

She had to be strong. If she couldn't erase the memory, neither could she erase the facts. That night had changed nothing between them. What happened in that bed had been based on exactly what she'd tried to convince him it had been: Need. Biology. Chemistry. And it couldn't happen again.

This...this new, semieasy truce they'd tentatively settled into—was a transition, a temporary cease fire until they returned to Jackson and got back to business as usual. Unfortunately it was almost more difficult to deal with his easy company than his sullen silence. Not as painful, but still difficult.

It was just another phase of the game, she decided as they both fell quiet and let the crackle of the fire replace conversation. First they'd tried to ignore that night, then they'd tried to ignore each other, and then they'd just flat-out pretended it had never happened by reminiscing about old times and revealing fantasies.

At least, she'd thought that's what they were doing, until the next words out of Clay's mouth blew her theory right out of the water.

"Is there any chance you could have gotten pregnant, Maddie?"

His soft question stunned her heart into beating so hard it almost cracked her ribs.

Assuring herself that if he could discuss it so matter-of-factly, she could, too, she willed her heart to steady.

"No. No chance." At least, she was relatively certain there wasn't. She wasn't on the pill nor did she rely on any other birth control devices. As a rule she didn't have to. Her bedroom didn't exactly have swinging doors, so protection wasn't a top priority. She was always aware of her cycles, however, and this was a safe time for her.

He nodded, seemingly content not to pursue that line of questioning. He wasn't, however, completely finished.

"I wasn't exactly prepared for what happened," he went on, "but I want you to know, you don't have to worry about me leaving you with anything else you don't want. I'm careful and I'm healthy." He lifted a shoulder, let it fall. "I thought maybe you'd want to know that. Set your mind at ease."

"I wasn't concerned," she said quickly.

The truth was she hadn't even thought about that aspect of their—for lack of a better word—encounter. With anyone but Clay she would have been cautious to a fault. Even though he'd been her nemesis for years, there was an innate integrity about him that she would never question. Just like she would never question that he would place her in any jeopardy.

"You don't have to worry, either," she added belatedly when it occurred to her that he may not have the same faith in her.

His soft, but sincere, "I wasn't," both warmed and relieved her.

She chanced a look at him then—just as he glanced over

at her. His lopsided smile was endearing. His blue eyes bold and inviting.

Oh, my, she thought and looked quickly away. She hugged a sofa pillow to her breast. Oh, my, could she get lost in those eyes again. Just like she could get lost in the dreamy idea of making love with him again. In wistful thoughts of what a beautiful baby she and Clay could make together. A baby like the one she wanted to have, to make her life complete.

Well, she couldn't afford to think about any of that. Not if they were going to salvage this tentative, fighting friendship that had taken such effort to rebuild. Not if she was going to make it through the next several days without begging him to take her back to bed.

This time when her instincts shouted "Run", she paid attention. When he touched a hand softly to her shoulder, she shot off the sofa like a bottle rocket on the Fourth of July.

"It's late," she announced abruptly and tugged her sweater down over her hips. "I'm tired. See you tomorrow."

Before he could so much as say good-night, she limped to the stairs and hightailed it up to the loft.

Clay scowled as he watched her go. He understood, of course. When their eyes had met and held for that brief moment, she'd felt the spark flare between them. She'd felt the sizzle and then left him here to deal with the burn.

It was, he admitted philosophically, the damnedest thing. She was everything he didn't want in a woman. Flighty, shrewish, unpredictable. And from the tone of her voice when she was reeling off her prerequisites for a husband, she didn't figure he fit any of her requirements, either.

He tugged on his lower lip and stared broodingly into the fire. He could be considerate. He was a decent person. He was respectful. He treated people like individuals and allowed them to be who they wanted to be. Apparently she didn't think so, though. But then, when had he ever shown her that side of himself?

Wildflowers. What kind of a woman preferred wildflowers to roses? Glazes to diamonds? And a horse? She'd rather be carried away on a horse than in a fancy foreign car?

Strange woman. But then, he'd always known that. Strange and stubborn and sassy and...sexy as ever-loving sin.

But she was not for him. No sir. He didn't care how hot she made his blood run. He didn't care that the night he'd spent with her in his arms was above and beyond any physical experience he'd ever shared with a woman.

You couldn't base a relationship on sex.... Stability. Accountability. Self-control. That's what built a solid relationship.

That fool woman was definitely not for him.

But then he'd always known that, too.

What he hadn't known...what he couldn't have ever guessed...was that she'd have the ability to make him sit there until three in the morning drilling himself on all of the reasons he shouldn't just climb on up those loft stairs and join her in that big old feather bed.

Eight

On the morning of the fifth day the rain was still falling. The cabin was getting smaller. The nights were getting longer. And both Maddie and Clay were feeling a frustration that stemmed as much from the enforced house arrest as from the sexual tension that built like flood waters behind a dangerously weakening dam.

On one thing, however, they were both determined. There would be no second act. No more searing love scenes. No encore performances.

To ensure that wouldn't happen, they took measures and pains to keep their physical contact to a minimum and their mission in perspective: wait it out, keep the peace, beat Garrett to a pulp *after* he'd led them back to Jackson and back to their individual lives.

While it helped to pass the time, they could only read so many books, play so many games of gin, checkers and Monopoly. The potential for physical contact was built in.

A brush of fingertips as they exchanged dice over the Monopoly board could shift from accidental contact to acute awareness and send their pulse rates skyrocketing. A squabble over a discarded card could trigger a physical tussle that started out with grins and giggles and ended up with long looks and elevated body temps.

The hardest for either of them to deal with, though, were the after-shower encounters. The scent of her shampoo arrested Clay. The sight of him still damp from the spray, barefoot and wearing nothing but his soft, faded jeans and smelling of shaving cream and toothpaste flooded Maddie's cheeks with color and set her nerve endings tingling. And for both of them, graphic memories of the night he'd bathed her and tended to her and held her and taken her to bed, shimmered on the edge of their consciousness like a vivid, erotic dream.

But for all the opportunities to stray into dangerous territory, it was the simple chore of cleaning up after breakfast one morning that brought things between them to a head.

The close quarters of the kitchen area always meant brushes of hip to thigh, shoulder to chest and conjured memories of bare skin and bold caresses. But it was an accident that incited the riot.

"You got my shirt wet," Clay sputtered as he stood by the sink, a dish towel in his big tanned hands.

Maddie glanced over her shoulder, her hands buried in breakfast dishes and soap suds. "Sorry."

Evidently she didn't sound sorry enough to suit him. "You did it on purpose."

She tilted her head and angled him a look. "My, we're testy this morning."

"You did it on purpose," he repeated looking surly and a little soggy and sounding a lot like a little boy who'd just had his balloon popped.

"I did not do it on purpose," she insisted feeling a little
testy herself. "And I said I was sorry."

She shot him a hard glare, then gathered two handfuls
of sudsy water and flung it directly at his chest. "I'm not
sorry about that, though. And it was definitely *not* an accident, so now you have something legitimate to pout
about."

Blue eyes darkened to cobalt and narrowed dangerously.
He looked from his drenched shirt to her. "I was *not* pout-
ing." Then he crowded up beside her, reached into the
soapy water and very deliberately soaked the front of her
T-shirt.

She sucked in a harsh breath, then growled long and low.
"You'll pay for that, James."

"Oh, yeah?" Crossing his arms over his chest, he glared,
superior and cocky, as she faced off with him. "And just
how—"

The contents of a full glass of water hit him squarely in
the face.

He clenched his jaw, then eyed her through the water
dripping from his hair. "Bad idea." Threat and malice
spiked both words.

Worse than bad, he realized as he stared at first her imp-
ish little smile, then made the mistake of lowering his gaze
to her wet shirt.

The soaking he'd given her made the thin material of her
white T-shirt transparent and clingy. A lacy scrap of a bra
showed through clearly —as did the full round curves of
her breasts and the delicate tips of her tightly puckered
nipples. Arousal spiked like a fever as he remembered the
taste of her. The velvety feel of her against his tongue.

Bucking a bolting desire to drag her against him and take
her into his mouth, wet shirt and all, he made himself stand
his ground, match her smile and gear toward retaliation.

"We can do this the easy way," he said, closing the

distance between them with one stalking stride, "or we can do it the hard way."

"Oh, by all means," she drawled, daring him with her eyes and her sassy mouth, "give it to me hard."

He clenched his teeth and smothered a groan as a traitorous part of his anatomy rushed to oblige her.

When he reached for her, she squealed, ducked and ran. She was fast. He was faster. He grabbed a fistful of her hair, slung his other arm around her waist, and spun her off her feet and back to the sink.

She shrieked, then laughed, then pleaded when he swung her up and onto the edge of the counter. "You wouldn't," she cried reading this thoughts through his eyes.

"Oh, but I would. And with great pleasure."

Then he picked her up and sat her right back down in the dishwater.

Bucking and gasping, she managed to not only splash water all over the counter and the floor but all over him as she launched herself out of the sink.

Instinct had him reaching out to steady her. Propulsion had her landing flush against his chest, her arms wrapped around his neck, her legs around his waist so the most intimate part of her was cuddling the most intimate part of him.

The impact and the sizzling contact knocked him off balance. He staggered backward, felt the front of a kitchen chair hit the back of his knees and sat down with a thud.

The aged pine strained, snapped, then crumpled under the impact and their combined weight, dumping them both on the floor.

That's where they stayed until Clay got his senses and his breath back. When he thought he had a loose handle on both, he lost it again when he realized his chest was full of woman and his hands were full of a lush wet bottom.

"You," he managed, as her shoulders shook with laughter, "are a disaster waiting to happen."

Disaster, it turned out, was the key word.

She slowly raised her head, then pushed herself up until she was sitting astride him. And as she sat there above him, her gypsy hair wild and tangled and tousled around her flushed, smiling face, he became grievously aware of how tempting she was.

There was the wet shirt to consider. It still wasn't doing much of a job concealing the shape of her breasts, the allure of her tight little nipples. And then there was her wet bottom.

Though his hands were no longer cupping her there—they'd shifted to the tiny curve of her waist—his palms still burned with the memory of how neatly she'd fit. She fit somewhere else just fine, too. Where her bottom connected with his groin, she pressed into him, soft and wet and wonderfully warm.

Suddenly she wasn't smiling anymore. And through her flashing dark eyes, he could see that water fights and getting even was the last thing on her mind.

Something far more compelling had shifted the flush of laughter on her face to beautiful, heated awareness. He searched her eyes, saw her need and knew nothing short of a natural disaster would keep him from fulfilling it.

"Come here," he demanded gruffly as he spread his fingers wide over the fine framework of her ribs and urged her unerringly toward him.

"This is a mistake," she whispered even as she bent to his mouth and let him draw her into a long, deep kiss.

"A big one," he murmured against her lips as he wrapped her tighter in his arms and rolled her beneath him. "And this one's mine...so now we're even."

With a shivery little sigh, she arched against his wan-

dering mouth as he trailed a string of nipping kisses down
her throat to her breast and sought her nipple.

She cried out, clutched handfuls of his hair. "So who's
keeping…oh, my God, do that again…who's keeping
score?"

"You are," he growled as he tugged her shirt out of her
jeans and peeled it over her head. "You are," he repeated
on a husky rumble as he unhooked the front clasp of her
bra, brushed the cups roughly aside and replace them with
his mouth, "and we both know it."

She would remember this, by God, Clay swore as he
drew her deeply into his mouth. He was going to make sure
of it. She was going to remember every touch, every caress,
every intimate demand his mouth and hands and body made
of hers.

When he'd made love to her before, he'd been gentle.
And she'd been sweet. Achingly so.

There was no gentleness in him now.

And there was no sweetness in her.

There was urgency and instant, white-hot greed.

"Off," she ordered, desperately working the buttons on
his shirt when he didn't do it fast enough to suit her. "Get
it off. I want to touch you."

He rose to his knees above her, his thighs straddling her
hips. To hell with the buttons. He ripped his shirt open and
was in the process of peeling it from his shoulders when
she arched up, clutched his thighs with her hands and
pressed hungry, biting kisses to his chest. He moaned when
she circled his nipple with her tongue then swore when her
busy, busy hands went to work on his belt buckle.

His abdominal muscles contracted involuntarily as the
back of her hands made tantalizing contact with bare flesh,
and his own hands knotted themselves loosely in her hair.

He'd never been in a tornado. Never experienced a hur-
ricane. But the force with which she demanded, the frenzied

speed with which she took, made him feel like he was
caught in one now.

Her hands were everywhere. Clawing down his back,
clutching his waist, streaking to his hips to cup and caress
and press him to her mouth to breathe fire against the strain-
ing bulge beneath his fly.

He groaned her name once, then again as he dragged her
away, lowered her to her back again on the floor. His arms
were shaking as he braced above her, his breath less than
steady as he pinned her hands above her head.

She strained against his grip like the waters of a wind-
tossed sea—all restless energy and impatient swells. Her
eyes were fever bright, burning into his, begging him to let
her have her way with him, begging him to have his way
with her. Her hair lay in a tangled, silky halo around her
beautiful bruised face. Her breasts, so pretty and pale, so
lush and full, rose and fell with her needy breaths, their
pink tips tightening in delicious response beneath the heat
in his gaze.

Demanding with his eyes that she watch him, he cupped
one breast possessively in his hand, electrified as much by
the way her eyes went dark as by the feel of her supple
flesh, the incredible velvet softness of her nipple. He'd
never known the simple act of touching a woman could
evoke longing this powerful. Or that the sight of the still-
angry bruise on her ribs could tear so sharply at his gut.

He released her hands, but not her gaze, caressed her
breast with the back of his knuckles, then let his hand slip
away. With a needful whimper she arched toward his touch.
Denying her, he slowly rose back to his knees.

She knew. She knew exactly what he wanted. Her eyes
never leaving his, she rose to her feet before him. Tangling
her hands in his hair, she tugged his head back and bent
over him. Enticingly, erotically she brushed the crest of her
breast across his waiting mouth. Seductively she lowered

her head, bowed her back, cocooning him with her body, the wild tumble of her hair, and the rush of sensations evoked by his seeking mouth.

She closed her eyes and let go of a breathless little moan. He could feast on the taste of her forever. And at the moment, that's all he wanted to do. He suckled, nipped, languidly licked then shaped her to the fit of his palms and began all over again. And she just kept on giving. Softly moaning, restlessly yearning, until the fire he'd ignited in them both burned out of control.

With a reckless cry, she pulled away, her eyes misty with longing, her breasts heaving as she finished the job she'd started on his fly. He returned the favor by unzipping, then stripping her jeans and silk panties roughly down her legs.

Then they were tangled in each other's arms again and she was pushing him to his back on the floor, flowing over him like a drape of silk, moving on him like a river. He lost himself in the texture of her skin, the woman curve of her hips, the dark desire in her eyes.

With hungry hands she surrounded him. With a shimmering sigh, she guided him home. And with the confidence of a woman pleasuring her man, she impaled herself on his heat then rode with him to a rhythm as wild as the mountains, as primitive as nature had ever intended.

She was grace and beauty. Fire and frenzy. And in that explosive moment before she seduced him over the exquisite edge where life ceased for a glorious instant, then began anew in a golden rush, two individual and distinctly different people became one. And in that moment it was only as one that they mattered.

Wholly wasted and devastatingly sated, Clay lay spread-eagle on his back on the hard, wood floor. He felt more dead than alive, yet more alive than he'd ever been in his life.

He was still breathing. That was a good sign. And slowly cognizant thought was making a comeback. Slower still, like walking against a strong wind or wading against a deep water current, it all came back. The reality of what just happened sank in.

The little gypsy had seduced him. Just like he hadn't yet caught his breath or regained enough strength to do anything but stare at the ceiling, he still couldn't quite believe it.

Oh, it had started innocently enough. And he'd been aware every step of the way that he was going to make love to her. But it was supposed to have been on his terms. It was supposed to have been under his control. Not that he was into dominance. He just wasn't into annihilation.

And that's exactly what she had done to him. He still wasn't sure when the shift from seducer to mindless putty had transpired. He only knew he didn't like it. At least he didn't think he liked it. Not the loss of control part, anyway. The other part—good Lord—the other was unbelievable.

When he heard her stir beside him, he rolled his head toward her. His first instinct was to reach for her and pull her close again. Despite the confusion he was feeling over what she'd managed to do to him, he would have acted on that instinct if she hadn't sat up, groped for her clothes and made a hasty retreat to the bathroom.

With a frown he watched her go. So much for a tender moment after.

With a deep breath, he crossed his hands behind his head and did a little more staring. And a lot more thinking.

What the hell is happening here? he wondered as he heard the spray of the shower hit the stall wall. *And why had it happened again?*

Even more puzzling, why had he let it?

Feeling his strength gradually restored, he rose and snagged his own clothes. He zipped up his jeans and shrugged into his shirt, frowning when he reached for buttons that were no longer there.

He scowled at the closed bathroom door, dismissed the fleeting thought that it would have been nice to join her.

"That would require an invitation, wouldn't it?" he muttered, suddenly angry as he opened the cupboard and snagged a mug for coffee.

Full mug in hand, he sat at the table, contemplated the broken chair and brooded about why he was suddenly in such a foul mood.

The reason was too obvious to discount. He'd been here. He'd done this. Once before they'd made fantastic, memorable love. And once before, she'd shut him out afterward. The first time it had been with excuses and words chosen carefully to ensure he'd back off. This last time she'd opted for the physical approach. She'd literally turned her back and shut herself off from him behind a closed door.

Well, he wasn't going to walk that road again. He wasn't going to let himself start thinking that they'd shared something other than sex. Something other than chemistry and physical need and another reckless moment.

Because that's obviously all this was to her.

A smart man would count his blessings and be damned glad she wasn't expecting something more from him than a quick, hot tumble. A smart man would be thanking the gods that he wasn't permanently entangled with a wild little gypsy like her.

"Damn," he muttered, dragging both hands down his face and wishing to hell and back that he was a smart man.

What timing. What absolute, ironic timing. It took a runaway woman, a mountain storm and another rash, reckless moment to figure out what his brothers had known all along.

He was in love with Maddie Brannigan. He was in love, damn his sorry hide. And damn her, she didn't have the good sense to love him back. Just like he had too much pride to let her know it.

He stared grimly out the window. If a bigger fool walked the earth, he'd like to meet him. They could have a good laugh at each other's expense.

When Maddie emerged from the bathroom a few minutes later, Clay couldn't help but feel that her intent had been to wash all traces of him clean from her body. She'd accomplished her goal in spades. Not only did she look squeaky clean beneath her clothes, all traces of hunger and heat and need had been stripped from her face. She couldn't have made her feelings clearer if she'd hung a sign around her neck that said Don't touch.

A chill as cold as the September rain rolled through his body.

Take it like a man, James, he told himself, and proceeded to do just that.

"Oops," he said, manufacturing a lopsided grin and giving a throwaway shrug of his shoulders. It was the best he could do by way of apology for his part in their little stray from grace. It was the best he could do because what he really wanted was to take her into his arms and start what they'd just finished all over again.

It was as plain as the heart on his sleeve, though, that she didn't want that. Looking skittish and embarrassed, she crossed her arms over her chest and looked at anything but him. "Yeah. Big oops."

While a very large part of him wished it could be otherwise between them, the sensible part accepted that it couldn't. He made himself clear the path for them to get on with the business of getting on. "Yeah. Well, accidents happen. Won't happen again, though—at least not that particular one."

"Right," she agreed stiffly. "It won't happen again."

He watched her face, foolishly looking for a sign, any sign, that she wasn't as sorry as she seemed to be. When none came, he bit the proverbial bullet and called that chapter closed.

He'd been fourteen when he'd lost his father. It had been hard, but he'd made it through that. He could tough this out, too. And even though his chest tightened at the thought of losing her, he could let her walk away.

What he couldn't do was stay in this cabin one more moment with nothing but her, nothing but memories of how she'd felt above him, how it felt to be inside her, dogging him like a shadow.

"Weather report," he said, forcing a cheerfulness he didn't feel, as he rose and rinsed his empty mug in the sink. "While we were, ah...otherwise occupied, the sun came out. Do I hear a hallelujah, sister?"

Her gaze drifted slowly to the window. Her unenthusiastic "Hallelujah" projected more relief than joy.

Because he couldn't conjure much of either, and because he couldn't look at her without wanting her, he left the kitchen without a word, found a shirt with all of its buttons and trudged outside.

Maddie let out several breaths that she hadn't been able to fully exhale since she'd found Clay in the kitchen all rumpled and mussed and looking like he was the one who'd been ravaged.

Lord, oh Lord, oh Lord. How had things gotten so messy again? How had she let what happened happen? Again.

And how could she live with this huge, hollow ache that threatened to burst inside her at the simple act of looking at him?

At his sexy, distant smile. At his thick black hair that felt like silk beneath her hands and that she would never touch again. At the sculptured muscle beneath his shirt that she'd never again caress or kiss. At the satin strength of his arms that she'd never, ever feel around her.

Somehow she had to figure out a way to deal with a loss that was never hers to bear. He had. And he hadn't pulled any punches. As far as he was concerned what they'd shared was just a big "Oops."

If she hadn't been hurting so much when he'd said it, she'd have liked nothing better than to have carved that snide little grin off his face with an extremely dull hacksaw. Make that a dull, rusty hacksaw.

"'Oops,' my sorry butt," she sputtered, and tried really hard to hate him.

Damn him. Damn, damn, damn him! He'd reduced what they'd shared to a mistake. To him, evidently, it was. Well, he'd never know that she thought otherwise. And he'd never know how much he'd hurt her. Both times....

She may be a little slow on the uptake, but she wouldn't be giving him another chance to get to her that way. There'd be no more fooling around. And no more feeling sorry for herself.

Resolved to deny the hurt, she climbed the loft stairs, only then realizing that their little scuffle on the floor had riled up her sore knee again. Limping in deference to the dull pain, she slowed her steps. Cabin fever or not, she would not set foot outside as long as he was out there.

"So what exactly are you going to do, champ?" she murmured as she reached the bedroom and realized she'd boxed herself in for the duration.

While the loft was sparsely furnished, it did boast a four-shelf bookcase crammed full of books. Grateful, but without enthusiasm, she browsed the selection. For some reason her attention kept wandering back to an ancient hardback volume on the James Gang.

"Outlaws, every one," she muttered, and thought morosely that all the James gang of old stole was money. The new generation stole hearts and then carelessly tossed them away.

"You are pathetic, Brannigan," she grumbled then selected the book out of spite to herself and flopped down on the bed.

Despite the fact that it promised to be interesting, she couldn't get into it. After rereading the first page three times, she tossed it on the quilt beside her and cursed herself one more time for being a melancholy sap.

She scrubbed her hands over her face, wincing when she touched her bruised temple—one more reminder of the results of the mess she was in. This whole episode in her life had been just one series of colossal boo-boos. The biggest boo-boo, she finally admitted, wasn't the physical damage she'd done. A damning tear leaked out and trickled from the corner of her eye and into her hairline. Her biggest mistake had been falling in love with Clay James.

Yep. That's exactly what she'd done. She'd fallen in love with the enemy, and there was as much chance of a thunderstorm in the desert as there was that he'd ever love her back.

Rolling to her side, she willed away the tears and stared at the book lying beside her on the bed. She ran her fingers over the cover, fiddled with the binding, opened it up again. It was when she was absently flipping through the pages that the key fell out.

Brows furrowed, she picked up the rusted skeleton key, studied it by the sunlight pouring in through the loft's cathedral window. She eased up on an elbow, looked from the key to the book. Picked up the book again. Slowly she opened it and discovered that the pages in the center had been cut out in exactly the shape of the key.

She touched the key again, her curiosity momentarily overshadowing her dark mood. Why would someone hide this key in this book? What did the key open?

It was in the midst of those tumbling questions that a story that Emma had told her came back with a rush and a little tingle of excitement.

A few minutes later she burst out the cabin door. The sun was welcome and high. The skies had cleared to a bachelor-button blue that showcased whipped cream clouds and the jagged mountain peaks.

With the key tucked securely in her pocket and her head full of a need to concentrate on something other than her stupid, pathetic heart, she headed for the river.

Love, Clay concluded after walking around for the better part of an hour, was for fools. That would explain, he admitted grimly, why he'd fall into it armpit deep.

As he headed back toward the cabin, he came to another conclusion. When love was one-sided, it was also for losers. Since he never played to lose and since there was no winning in this particular game, he made another decision. If he could fall in love with Maddie Brannigan, he could, by God, fall out of it.

The sooner, the better. As hard as it was to admit, he didn't think he could live with this aching sense of loss for very long.

Starting now, he was getting over her. Starting now, his heart wouldn't feel like it was being squeezed by a punishing fist at just the sight of her. Yet when he rounded the back of the cabin, saw her limping down the cabin steps, and felt that squeeze as acutely as a physical touch, he accepted that getting over her might not be quite as simple as he wanted it to be.

He stopped where he stood, partially hidden by the cover of the forest, watching her, aching for her, and wondered what the hell the fool woman was up to now.

When she made a beeline for the river, he scratched his head, frowned and then stalked after her—not because he couldn't stay away from her. He could have done that if he'd wanted to. He could have just watched her walk away, not moved at all by the way the sunlight glanced off her springy curls. Not affected in the least by her comical little gait as she limped along favoring her knee.

And he didn't stall a twinge of sympathy for her poor bruised knee. What he did manage was to curse her wardrobe and wonder why there couldn't ever be any middle ground with her. Either she wore those ugly, baggy sweaters and long, flowing skirts that hid her sweet, delectable figure, or her tidy little butt was encased in short shorts or snug jeans that showcased every sassy curve.

Like now. Hers isn't the only sexy behind in Jackson Hole, he assured himself grumpily as he kept on her trail and willed himself not to think about peeling those damn jeans off her and dragging her back to the cabin and to bed.

He told himself he could turn around and head back anytime he chose to. He promised himself that the only reason he was following her was because he was curious about what she was up to.

By the time she reached the river and it became apparent she wasn't going to slow down as she followed its snaking path north, he didn't have to work so hard on the convincing part. By now he really was curious—and a little concerned. The woman tempted trouble wherever she went, and he sure as the world wasn't up for another rescue from the edge of a cliff.

Enough was enough. He trotted to catch up with her. "Maddie!"

His yell startled her into stopping.

She spun around, her black eyes wide, her hand pressed to her heart.

Her shoulders sagged in relief when she saw it was him. Her voice, when she found it, sounded breathless and airy. "You scared the begezes out of me."

"What the hell are you up to?" he demanded brusquely when he reached her side.

Her chin lifted. "Treasure hunting."

He scowled, tilted his head, and when comprehension dawned, worked really hard on a condescending snort. "So you found out about the gold, did you?"

"Yeah," she said, and started marching again. "I found out about the gold."

Nine

Maddie couldn't do it. She couldn't stand there beside him, his blue eyes boring into hers, his big body just inches away, and not hurt from wanting to touch him.

She couldn't stop the hurt but she could do her damnedest to keep him from seeing it. Head down, determined to concentrate on her mission, she started walking again. "Emma told me about it."

It didn't surprise her when he fell into step beside her. She just wished it didn't kick her heart into the Wyoming equivalent of a Texas two-step.

"And what, exactly, did she tell you?"

He wasn't going away. Deal with it, she told herself and kept right on walking. "Word for word or just the outline?"

"Oh, by all means, let's hear the whole story—see how much it's grown in the telling."

She had no doubt he knew the story inside out, upside

down and backward. But because it was easier to talk than endure the memories the silence courted, she obliged him.

"According to Emma, who got her information from Garrett, your ancestors, Frank and Jesse James, hid out in this valley after they'd robbed a train in Arkansas and made off with a fortune in gold. They'd settled here, at this bend of the Wind River, thinking they were safe, when a posse tracked them down several months later. Taken by surprise, they lit out in a hurry and left their loot behind. Right so far?"

He tucked his hands in his hip pockets and kept pace beside her. "As right as a tall tale can be."

His comment surprised her. "You mean you don't believe the story?"

He shrugged. "As a kid I believed every word. Dad used to love to tell it and speculate about where the gold was hidden. I suspect, though, that what he was really doing was getting us boys out of his hair for a while—sending us on a wild-goose chase so he could spend some quiet time with Mom."

He paused, smiled, remembering. "It worked, too. We used to spend hours combing the valley, the foothills, the riverbanks."

"But never finding," she concluded, remembering him as a boy, tall and gangly back then, his quick grin reckless and ornery.

"You can't find what's not there."

"Are you forgetting the gold coin Emma and Garrett found in the river this summer?"

Clay had almost forgotten about that. And while he discounted the tale of the chestful of gold as folklore, in truth, he did find it more than coincidental that they'd found the old coin in this very area—in fact, in the very bend of the river they'd just reached.

"A lot of settlers crossed the river here," he said, willing to explain it away. "Could have dropped out of any number of pockets."

"Just like the old gun handle and the rusted hinge that could have come from a lock box?" she added referring to the boxful of "treasures" the brothers had found as boys and had pinned their hopes on.

"Just like," he said, disputing the challenge in her voice.

"So what you're saying," she said slowly, speculatively, "is that Clay James, the boy, was a dreamer but that Clay James the man is a skeptic."

He rolled his shoulders. Squinted into the warmth of the sun. He'd sure been dreaming when he'd hoped her feelings for him ran as deep as his did for her. She'd given him more than enough reason to be a skeptic.

"The man is a realist," he said finally. "Hidden treasure, Spider-Man and mermaids were a part of my misspent youth," he finished with a smile meant to convince them both that he had no emotional investment in the gold or in her.

"Well, I hope I never become that cynical," she stated resolutely. "Or that skeptical."

Or that grounded, he added silently, and tried to count himself lucky again. Everything she'd said so far fit his perception of her. She was a dreamer. It went with her artist's soul. And it was just one more reason why he was better off without this little gypsy messing up his neat and tidy life.

"What about the shell casing?" she continued, unwilling to give it up. "The one with the note inside?"

Explain that, her raised chin and determined look seemed to say. Evidently Emma had been thorough in relating the details.

Again he had to admit that the shell, too, was a puzzle. During Garrett and Emma's stay at the cabin this past summer, Emma had noticed an old tintype of Frank James that had been passed down generation after generation. In the picture Frank wore a leather thong around his neck. Attached to the thong was a spent shell casing. The casing looked similar to one that the boys had found years ago and kept in their special cache of mementos along with the gun handle and rusted hinge.

When Garrett and Emma had hunted up that shell and cracked it open, they'd found a tiny roll of brittle paper inside. On the paper were letters that Emma was certain were clues to the location of the gold.

"Can't explain that away, can you?" Maddie said, nudging him back to the moment.

Again he shrugged. "I opt for Garrett's theory. The letters could have been anything from a grocery list to an address. Or they could have been of no significance at all. And it's a real stretch to assume it was the same shell Frank wore around his neck."

"You have no sense of adventure," she insisted gravely. "And for whatever reasons, you're looking past the obvious."

He would liked to enjoy the look on her face. The way she was warming to the challenge of proving him wrong, playing out the fantasy, building on her beliefs. But that would have been indulging. He couldn't afford to indulge. Not in her.

"I think Emma's explanation fits perfectly. The letters, though old and faded, clearly said 'WISKY ROC.' Whisky Rock," she restated emphatically when he didn't say anything. "Just like that rock over there."

His gaze followed hers to the bank of the river and the boulder that had held so much significance to Emma and now, apparently, to Maddie, too.

The rock was big and brown and without employing too much imagination, it did resemble a whisky bottle lying on its side.

"Emma was right," she continued. "The note and that rock are tied to the gold."

"The only thing significant about that rock is that all three of us boys carved our initials on its side." He walked over to the boulder, ran a fingertip along the artless *C.J.* scratched between Garrett's and Jesse's initials.

"And I suppose there's no meaning to this, either?" More than a trace of smugness colored her tone when she produced a rusty key and held it out for him to inspect.

He frowned and, careful not to touch her, lifted the key from her palm. He turned it to the sunlight. "Where'd you come up with this?"

When she told him, he rubbed his chin, sniffed.

"What's the matter, Clayton? This little turn got you stumped?"

"Puzzled," he admitted. "You say it was an old volume on the James Gang?"

She rattled off the date on the author's note and then added the clincher. "By my calculations the book was printed just before Frank and Jesse's last big robbery. The one where they stole that gold shipment."

"And you've decided that book belonged to Frank or Jesse?"

"More than one infamous character has collected scrapbooks or memorabilia about their lives."

He still wasn't buying it. "It still wouldn't explain why it turned up here. Or what that key opens."

"I can't explain how the book ended up in your cabin, either," she admitted. "That part's got me stumped. But I'd bet my mother's pearls that it opens a strongbox full of gold."

He snorted and settled a hip on the part of the rock that looked like the bottle's neck. "You don't lack for imagination, I'll give you that."

When she didn't reply with a smart, snippy remark, he

finally granted himself license to indulge in one thing he'd been trying to avoid. He looked at her. At her wild curls, her sensual mouth, those sultry, brown eyes—and the look of discovery bursting over her face like a sunrise.

"What?" He stood slowly, reacting to her sudden, building excitement. "You look like you just saw a ghost."

"No ghost." Her voice was breathless with anticipation. "But maybe a ticket to the gold. Look." She pointed to the boulder.

He didn't see anything and said as much.

"No, no. Really look," she insisted when he wrinkled up his brow and scowled. "The rock. Whisky Rock. There's more than your initials carved in the stone. Here. And here," she cried, outlining a fainter, paler etching directly underneath the ones they had made as boys.

"You probably never noticed it because all you saw was your initials. Can you see it now? There's a five and a zero. And here, see it? It's an *S.* Fifty S," she concluded breathlessly and got down on her knees to trace the remaining scratches with her fingers.

Clay couldn't do anything but watch her, captivated by her excitement and her energy and at the same time dubious of her supposed discovery.

"Thirty E," she announced, deciphering a second set of scratchings and quickly moved on to the last. "Fifteen S." Her brow pinched in thought and then decision. "Fifty S, Thirty E, Fifteen S. Oh, my God. Directions. Clay—they carved directions in the boulder! Directions to where they hid the gold. Fifty S is fifty paces south, Thirty E is thirty paces east, Fifteen S, fifteen paces south again."

She scrambled to her feet. "It's a map. Frank and Jesse left a map so that when they came back here, they could remember where they hid the gold. Only they never made it back.

"But we did," she cried, her dark eyes flashing as she

literally bounced in place, all energy and expectation. Like she looked when they made love, he thought as a shaft of desire speared through him.

"All we have to do is follow them, find the gold and take it home.

"Why are you just standing there?" she demanded with an impatient flap of her hands. "Why aren't you excited?"

He was excited all right. Only it wasn't for the same reasons she was all riled up. *She* excited him. The childlike way she embraced her wild-hare conclusions. The womanly way she filled out her shirt and jeans. And woven through it all was the memory of her beneath him, surrounding him, sighing for him, only him, when she shattered like glass in his arms.

The wanting to take her here, again, in the sunlight, with the mountains as witness and the sky as silent counsel, had him stuffing his fists in his pockets to keep from reaching for her. He'd fought stronger urges in his life. Surely he had. Right now he couldn't remember when—and he'd never staged a battle this important with so little heart in it. Just like he'd never won a fight that held such a small sense of victory.

"Why aren't you excited?" she repeated, demanding he join in on the action and the adventure.

He shook his head to clear it of thoughts of her. "Because you've put three and three together and come up with a whopping one hundred, that's why," he said with as much calm in his voice as he could level. "Because a musty old piece of paper tucked in a shell casing and a few scratches on a boulder don't a treasure map make."

An adamant shake of her head told him she wasn't going to let him douse her fire. "Well, Mr. 'Mired in Absolutes,' who's to say I'm any more wrong than you are right? Who's to say three and three doesn't add up to one hundred in this case? Or one thousand? Or a hundred thousand?

"Are you afraid, Clayton?" she asked after a moment. "Are you afraid to take a chance? To have a little fun? To color outside the lines for just once in your life and see if maybe, just maybe there really might be a pot of gold at the end of this rainbow?"

He tightened his lips into a grim, hard line and when he couldn't hold it in the face of her feisty little challenge, he let a crooked grin take over. "Why, if I didn't know better, Matilda, I'd swear you just issued a dare."

"You're darn right I did. There's a chest of gold out there somewhere, and I'm of a solid mind to find it. Are you with me or do I go it alone?"

Because he was slowly coming to realize he'd have a hard time denying her anything and because the prospect of her sassy stubborn self traipsing around the valley alone threatened a major heart attack, he gave her the only answer he could.

"Oh, I'm with you, hotshot. I wouldn't have it any other way."

"We found it. Oh. My God. We actually found it."

Maddie's voice was barely a whisper as, she and Clay gazed at the aged, locked strongbox they'd just unearthed from beneath a pile of rocks.

They knelt side by side on the damp, dank, dirt floor of a cave they'd discovered less than fifteen minutes ago. The entrance had been all but obscured by dense undergrowth and carefully positioned boulders.

It was the afternoon of the sixth day—a grueling twenty-four hours after Maddie had deciphered the etchings on Whisky Rock. Several false starts and dead ends had left Maddie with a sprained ankle to go with her bruised knee and another scratch on her cheek to go with her black-and-blue temple.

Clay hadn't fared much better. Thanks to Maddie's elbow accidentally connecting with his eye when he'd caught her in a near fall, a beefsteak the size of Texas couldn't have helped his shiner. His right eye was practically swollen shut to the complement of black, blue, purple and a hint of murky green.

At the moment neither of them were conscious of their cuts and contusions as they stared in stunned awe at their find.

While they'd been in agreement that Whisky Rock was their starting place, it was Clay who had finally concluded that they needed to mark their pace from the bottom of the bottle, not the top. And now it was Clay, who'd merely been humoring her, who ate a little humble pie.

"*We* didn't do it," he said generously. "You did. I was only tagging along to make sure you didn't get yourself killed."

"It doesn't matter," she insisted as she latched on to one of the strongbox's handles and tugged. "Let's get it out into the light and get it open."

It was no easy feat. The box was approximately two feet long and a foot high and deep. And it weighed a small ton. When they finally managed to drag it out of the cave, Maddie plopped down tiredly on her rump and just marveled at it.

"Look. A hinge is missing. I'm betting the other one is back in the cabin."

Clay only grunted and fussed with the rusty lock.

"What about you? Wanna bet on whether or not this fits?" Brimming with smiles, she produced the key from her pocket and held it out to him.

He leaned back on his haunches. "You made the find. You do the honors."

Biting her lower lip, she inched closer to the locked box. Her fingers trembled with excitement as she inserted the key into the padlock.

"It fits." Her breathless exclamation gave away that she'd had her reservations, too. "It actually fits."

With her breath caught in anticipation, she turned the key, then frowned when it wouldn't budge and tried again.

"It's rusted tight," Clay said after he'd tried the lock, too. "We'll have to break into it."

Maddie was too excited to do anything but watch as Clay picked up a stone about the size of his fist. Using it like a hammerhead, he gave the lock a good rap. After two more solid hits, and a skinned knuckle, it gave way.

"This is it," he said after letting out a deep breath. "Open it up, Maddie. Let's have a look."

Eyes wide with excitement, cheeks flushed with anticipation, she slowly lifted the lid—then stared in fascinated silence at what she found inside.

After sharing a puzzled look with Clay, she reached first for the single gold coin lying on top of a boxful of coarse river sand.

"I don't understand." She looked from the coin to the sand-filled box.

Clay reached for a flat leather pouch wedged under the metal braces in the lid of the box. "Maybe this will explain something."

He opened the small packet and pulled out a sheet of age-yellowed paper that wore the unmistakable scent of mold.

The inked letters were smudged but readable:

"A fool's treasure is gold. A wise man's treasure is sweeter. It starts and ends with home. J. James."

He handed the note to Maddie, not entirely surprised when she smiled through her initial disappointment, then got all misty-eyed.

"How beautiful. And how poetic. What do you suppose it means?"

He shook his head. "You got me."

He watched her face while she reread the note, still clutching the coin in her hand. "Disappointed?"

She shrugged. "Not really," she said and he could see that she meant it. "Intrigued," she allowed. "Mystified," she added and frowned down at the strongbox. "And while I can't help but wonder about where the rest of the gold went, it was the hunt that was exciting. The find that was the real reward."

She squinted against the sun, then looked into his eyes. "We made a pretty good team, didn't we?"

"Yeah," he said, his voice rusty with regret that she didn't feel they could team up in any other aspect of their lives.

He looked from her beautiful, battered face and checked the sky. "It's getting late. We'd better take our treasure," he nodded toward the coin with a grin, "and head for the cabin before dark sets in."

"This is rightfully yours." She offered him the gold.

He folded his hand around hers, closing her fingers into a small, delicate fist. "You found it. You keep it. It was never mine, anyway."

Just like she would never be his.

In a pensive silence, edged with any number of regrets, they made the hike back to the cabin.

Garrett would come for them tomorrow. Garrett would come, they would return to Jackson and everything would return to the status quo.

So Maddie told herself as she sat before the fire and ordered herself to go to bed. Alone. Soon.

It would have to be soon or she was going to fold like a tent in a high wind and beg Clay to make love to her again.

It was the oldest cliché in the world. And the loneliest. Unrequited love. No...she didn't have his love, but she still had some remnants of her pride. It was that pride that finally had her rising from the sofa without a word and heading toward the loft stairs.

She sensed Clay's gaze on her from where he sat in an overstuffed chair, broodily engrossed in the fire. Sensed that he wanted to say something. Something appropriate to end their seven-day exile. Something like, Thank God it'll be over tomorrow. Something like, It's been an experience. It's been a drag. It's been a long time coming to an end.

But he said nothing and neither did she. Only the creak of the loft stairs beneath her feet accompanied her leaving him there. Only the wind, rustling through the pine outside the loft bedroom window acknowledged her presence as she slipped out of her clothes, into a nightshirt and slid between the covers.

And only the moon, shining like a spotlight, witnessed the silent tears she shed, then angrily wiped away.

"Self-pity is for the pitiful," she recited in a firm whisper. They were words from her mother, words from her childhood, and they echoed like her beating heart through the night.

It was a night that never seemed to end as she lay awake, listening to the sound of her own breathing, the keen edge of loneliness and the hollow prospect of a future without the man she loved sighing into the darkness.

She knew it was over. She knew it had never really started. Somehow, though, she had expected that whatever it was that hadn't really happened between them wouldn't have ended in silence. She'd expected a bang. An explosion of sound and emotion. A battle royal that said it wasn't easy to give up on the possibility of there being something more.

But the truth was it was something less. Something that was as easy for him to let go of as daylight. As easy as passing from midnight to morning.

* * *

Below, in the silent cabin, Clay stared into the dark. Somewhere around midnight, he rose and went to bed.

He didn't sleep. Arms folded beneath his head, he, too, stared into the darkness. He, too, felt the sting of loneliness like a slap to his peace and his hopes and his dreams.

Dreams. Funny. He'd never thought of himself as a dreamer. Not until he'd fallen in love with one. Not until he'd experienced the unpleasant prospect of losing what he'd never known he needed most in his life.

Morning brought sunshine and surliness.

Exhausted from lack of sleep and cranky from a sadness that had settled bone deep, Maddie threw things into her duffel, her mood as foul as any storm had ever thought about being.

Outside, grumpy as a grizzly separated from its meal, burned out from a sleepless night, Clay stalked around pulling the water line, draining the pump and winterizing the generator.

Maddie didn't want to go outside and run into him.

Clay didn't want to go back inside and face her.

She tidied up the cabin and looked toward the ridge, telling herself Garrett couldn't get here soon enough.

He locked up the toolshed, glared toward the ridge and wondered what in the hell was taking Garrett so long.

Neither wasted any time gathering their gear. They were waiting on the porch in dead silence when two riders with two packhorses and two riding horses in tow cleared the small gully between river and cabin. By the time Garrett and Jesse reined up in front of the porch, Maddie and Clay were both feeling meaner than a twenty-four-hour bug and just as toxic.

Garrett stared at the two of them, then at Jesse with grim-

mouthed wonder. Jesse just tugged his hat low over his eyes
and braced his hands on the pommel of his saddle.

Garrett wasn't sure what he'd expected. He only knew
what he'd hoped. He'd hoped to see two people silly and
sappy in love.

He saw soured and stone faces instead. And blood.

Oh, Lord. He actually saw blood.

What he could see through the bruising and swelling,
showed that the white of his brother's left eye was lost in
a sea of red. The fingers of his left hand wore a white
bandage dotted with seeping blood.

Garrett swallowed hard, dragged his gaze from Clay to
Maddie and felt his stomach drop to his knees. Her temple
was black and blue, her face was scratched, and—he gulped
and let out a devastated breath—she limped when she carefully maneuvered the porch steps.

That's when he saw the pieces of a broken chair stacked
with the firewood on the porch.

What had they done to each other?

*And what, in heaven's name, had he done when he'd left
them here alone?*

The trip back to Jackson Hole was eventful only because
of the lack of events.

They rode in absolute silence. Garrett and Jesse were
afraid to break what might have been the only buffer between peace and full-out war. Clay and Maddie simply
didn't have anything to say. Nothing that could change
things, at any rate.

When they finally reached town and Maddie's apartment,
Garrett and Jesse quickly jumped down, grabbed her gear
and hustled it inside and up the stairs.

Only then, when they were alone outside, with the sun
just settling in for another night beyond the Tetons, did
Maddie acknowledge that Clay had something to say.

"Spit it out," she said as he stood in an uneasy silence beside her. "It's just going to eat at you if you don't."

His one good eye was kind, almost wary, as he finally met hers. "No regrets, right?"

There in the twilight she felt herself sway slightly toward him and made herself look away. "No regrets."

Another heavy moment passed and he touched a hand to her shoulder. "And you're sure—" he paused, tipped back his head, let out a deep breath "—you're sure there's no chance you could have gotten pregnant?"

His face relayed both his concern and how uncomfortable he was, asking. She supposed she should have felt grateful. Instead she felt a cutting pain, a desolate loss. He was concerned, yes. Concerned for his neat and tidy little life and how an unplanned and unwanted pregnancy could mess it up.

It hurt to think that the possibility of a baby was so repugnant to him. But life hurt sometimes, and there was nothing she could do to avoid it. She could, however, keep what was left of her pride from eroding.

"No," she assured him and prayed the heartache didn't show in her eyes or her voice. "There is absolutely no chance that I'm pregnant."

Ten

She was pregnant.

At first she hadn't known whether to laugh or cry or rail at poor Maxwell who sat in the corner of her studio, his tail snapping in concert with Maddie's frantically spinning potter's wheel.

That was at first. That was when she was scared and stunned and had finally accepted that three separate brands of home pregnancy tests couldn't be wrong. That was also in October, one and a half months ago. Since then she'd had it confirmed by her GP who had referred her on to an OB clinic.

It hadn't taken all seventy-five days for her to embrace the idea that she was having a baby. It had taken all of one. One emotionally draining, soul-searching, grinning-like-a-goon day to realize that nothing, absolutely nothing could make her happier than the prospect of having a child of her own.

Well, nothing short of having a child with a man who loved her.

"But, hey...you can't have everything, right Max?"

Disgruntled by the noise of her spinning wheel, Max leaped up to his bed in the sunny window and turned his back on her.

"Men," she mumbled with a halfhearted grin and set about convincing herself how lucky she was.

It was two weeks until Christmas. There was snow on the ground and a fire in her hearth. Her new gallery was beautiful and more successful than ever. Her studio was state-of-the-art, and her loft apartment above the gallery was spacious and airy. She was already making plans to turn one of her two spare bedrooms into a nursery.

"It'll be fun when I can share my plans with someone," she said aloud as she critically studied the piece she'd just crafted. "No offense, Max, but you're just not that good with wallpaper and fabric swatches."

Rising slowly, she stretched, washed her hands, then rubbed at the dull ache in her lower back.

"Nothing to be concerned about," Dr. Moyer had assured her. "But I don't want to see you bending over that wheel for half a day then spending another four to six hours on your feet in the gallery. You've got to slow down the pace."

He hadn't had to tell her twice. The first month had taken a toll on her stamina. Once she was past that, the morning sickness had hit. She'd never been good at being sick, and she was glad that particular little element of gestation was, for the most part, behind her. Now the leg cramps were giving her fits at night.

"But we're handling it, right Max?"

Yeah. She was handling it so well, she was reduced to rambling to her cat.

When the bell over the gallery door rang, she tugged off

her smock and smoothed her hands over her tummy, which was just hinting at producing a little bulge. Thankful for her penchant for loose sweaters, she headed toward the sound.

"Anybody home?" Emma's voice rang through the gallery to the studio.

"Em," she cried, breaking into a huge grin.

She zipped through the studio door and rushed headlong into Emma's arms for a long, clinging hug.

When she pulled away, she was smiling through tears, and Emma was clearly wondering what the devil was going on.

"Are you okay?" she asked carefully.

Realizing belatedly that her emotional display was a bit overblown when she'd just seen Emma the day before, she backpedaled with a nervous laugh. "I'm fine. Geez. It's almost Christmas. I guess I've caught the spirit."

"I guess," Emma said, smiling now, too, but with guarded concern. "Are you sure you're okay? You've seemed sort of...I don't know. Emotionally fragile the past few weeks."

Maddie forced a laugh. "Oh, for heaven's sake. I haven't been fragile—emotionally or physically—since I found out there wasn't a Tooth Fairy."

Then, without warning, the tears—a whole bucket of them—gushed through the hole she'd been patching with determination and stubborn pride. "And there isn't, you know," she sobbed as a totally perplexed Emma James placed a consoling arm over her shaking shoulders.

"There isn't what, sweetie?"

"A Tooth Fairy," she wailed, through a hiccuping sob. "There's no To-oth Fairy, and there's n-no, Easter B-Bunny, and, and, there's no S-Santa Claus!"

"Oh, Maddie, honey," Emma crooned as she folded her

friend in her arms and wondered what in the world was going on.

Worried and dumbfounded, she stood there rocking her, absorbing her tears on the collar of her coat and racking her brain for understanding.

"Oh, my Lord," she murmured abruptly, when she put together Maddie's recurrent bouts of "stomach flu," the slight flush to her cheeks, the sense that she was always hovering on the brink of an emotional edge. And now this.

"Maddie," she said, gently setting her at arm's length. "You're pregnant, aren't you?"

Maddie blinked once, then sniffled through an outraged, "Who told you?"

Emma couldn't help it. She laughed. Then she hugged her again. "You did, sweetie. Only I wasn't listening until the bad news about the Tooth Fairy broke your heart."

All the tension suddenly eased from Maddie's shoulders, like the weight of the Tetons had just been lifted. She managed a teary little smile and then a self-derisive laugh.

"Am I going to be like this all nine months?" She blew her nose on the tissue Emma offered.

"On and off," Emma conceded and led her back toward the studio where she knew Maddie had taken to keeping a pot of herbal tea brewing. She poured them both a cup. "But you'll learn to read the signs and keep it under control."

Behind the closed door of the studio, Emma regarded her with concern. "Do you want to tell me about it?"

This was the part Maddie had been both hoping for and dreading.

"Not much to tell," she said with a slight lift of her shoulders.

"Let's start with When are you due? How are you feeling?"

"I'm due in May and for the most part, I'm feeling

fine." Her smile was bittersweet. "I remember asking you those same questions a couple of months ago."

"I'm so happy for you, Maddie."

"Me, too." She pinched back another threat of tears. "Darn, I hate this. I blubber and bawl at the most stupid things."

"Stupid things like worrying about how you're going to handle all this by yourself?" Emma suggested gently.

When Maddie hung her head, Emma pressed on. "Have you told the baby's father?"

Suddenly Maddie's cup of tea captured all of her attention.

"I don't want to be judgmental," Emma said after a moment to digest that Maddie's silence was a negative answer, "but don't you think it's a little unfair to keep him in the dark?"

"He doesn't want the baby," she stated uncategorically. "He doesn't want me."

Emma's frown was probing. "So you *have* told him."

Fidgety suddenly, Maddie rose and walked to the window. "No. No, I haven't told him. But I know what he'd say. I know what he'd do."

"And what would that be?"

"He'd insist we get married," she said as if that were the equivalent of being boiled in oil.

"This would be bad?" Emma prodded in that same gentle tone.

"It would be very bad. I'm not going to trap someone who doesn't love me into marrying me."

"And why are you so sure he doesn't love you?"

Her laugh was short and harsh. "You'll have to trust me on this one."

"What about you? Do you love him?"

Squaring her shoulders, Maddie stared at the snow-capped mountains in the distance and made her voice as cold as those jagged peaks. "How I feel about him doesn't matter much, does it? Besides, I wouldn't turn to him if he was the last lifeboat leaving a sinking ship."

"Oh, Lord," Emma murmured as her second revelation of the day hit her right between the eyes. "It's Clay."

Emma James appeared the picture of gentile Southern-bred sugar, but she was as determined as a jackhammer when she was grounded in conviction. And she was convinced that Maddie owed it to herself and to the baby and to Clay to tell him.

A week later, Emma finally wore Maddie down. She'd be showing soon, anyway, Maddie reasoned grudgingly. Clay may have been avoiding her like she was Typhoid Mary since they'd returned from Wind River in September, but she was bound to run into him in a town the size of Jackson. Even if their paths didn't cross, word would eventually get around. He wasn't stupid. He had ten fingers and a calendar. Sooner or later he'd figure it out. In the end she decided she'd rather he find out on her terms than by chance.

That's why she'd driven out to the site of the James boys' current project on this snowy December afternoon and was in the process of marching across the construction site looking for Clay.

The sun was hidden behind a heavy quilt of snow-laden clouds. Huge, fluffy flakes drifted like lace pinwheels, promising to add another inch or two to the pristine layer of white by nightfall. Tugging the collar of her wool jacket tighter around her neck, Maddie picked her way around piles of lumber and walked toward the pickup truck she recognized as Clay's.

When she saw him, her footsteps slowed. Her heart, on the other hand, picked up several beats. She'd held a picture in her mind of how he'd looked the day they'd parted ways in September. His dark hair had fallen rakishly over his forehead, his poor battered eye had been narrowed against the setting sun, his shoulders were broad and squared with impatience to be rid of her.

She'd thought she was prepared to see him again after that day almost three months ago. She'd thought a lot of things. She'd never thought she'd be standing here in the snow looking at him—glad for the moment that he was unaware of her presence—and thinking about how lucky her baby was to have drawn from a gene pool that produced such stunning beauty.

And, oh, was he beautiful. She ached from wanting to touch him again, to be touched by him. To go to him, have him enfold her in his arms and welcome the news she was about to share.

But she didn't, and he wouldn't. So she just studied him in profile as he stood by the truck, one booted foot hooked on the running board, an elbow propped on the rail of the truck bed. He spoke into a cell phone, calmly and systematically relaying instructions to a crew member who was evidently working at a different site.

"That should do it," he said, then tipped back his head and laughed in response to something the other person said. "Okay, bud. I'll catch you later."

He disconnected and tucked the palm-size phone into the breast pocket of his quilted flannel vest. Then, as if he sensed someone was watching him, he froze for an almost indiscernible moment before turning slowly toward her.

She couldn't help it. She looked for a sign—any sign— that he might be glad to see her. That he'd missed her. That he, too, had lain awake at night, wanting her, needing her. But the soft smile that had lingered from his phone conversation melted to the equivalent of leery curiosity before transitioning to an outright scowl.

So much for fantasy. And so much for hope.

"Maddie," he said, his voice not sounding exactly harsh, but distant enough that she wrapped her coat protectively over her tummy. "What are you doing way out here?"

Oh, boy. Did she have an answer for that one. *Why, I came to change your life forever,* seemed the most concise way to explain her presence, but she couldn't quite muster the courage to blurt it out.

"How's it going, Clay?" she said instead, playing for time, stalling the inevitable.

"Fine," he said, his brows lowering over blue eyes gone dark with a wary suspicion. "And you? How are things with you?"

"Fine," she said on a heavy sigh. "Just…fine."

He stared at her for a moment longer, propped a hand on his hip and absently rubbed a spot over his left eye. "Something I can do for you, Maddie?"

This was it. She swallowed back the lump of apprehension and gave it a shot. "Actually—"

The tinny ring of his cell phone cut her off.

"Sorry." He fished out the phone and punched the connection. "Clay here."

With her heart still stalled somewhere in the vicinity of her throat, she practiced some deep breathing exercises to settle herself down, then jumped at the sound of his voice.

"You can't be serious," he shouted into the phone. "No, no…I'm not blaming you. Damn," he muttered after a moment, then shook his head. "We've got to have those struts. Don't let him leave. Just stall him until I get there." He flicked his wrist, checked his watch. "Give me ten minutes." Even as he disconnected, he was sprinting around the cab and climbing inside.

"Sorry, Maddie," he called as he turned the ignition and slammed into gear. "I'll give you a call later, okay?"

Then he was off, pealing out of the lot before she could decide if she felt relieved, irritated or just plain adrift.

"Reprieves aren't all they're cracked up to be," she mumbled as she tracked back to her car and made the return trip to her gallery.

She felt kind of like she was all dressed up with no place to go. And she hadn't dressed up for nothing. No matter how much it hurt, no matter how much pride was invested, before the day was over, Clayton James was going to know he was going to be a father. And then he was going to find out the rules according to Maddie Brannigan.

Agnes Crawford was clearly curious but patient when Maddie called the James Construction Company's main office for the second time that day to ask where she could find Clay.

With the address in hand, Maddie drove to yet another job site. As he had been earlier, Clay was a combination of frowning suspicion and guarded curiosity. And just like the last time, he got called away before she could spit out her statement, lay down her rules and leave him to figure out that she didn't intend to infringe on his life.

By three o'clock that afternoon, she'd reached her limit. And as far as she was concerned, he'd lost two opportunities. Since he was so darn good at dealing with crises over the phone, she figured one more wouldn't hurt.

"This's Clay," he answered on the second ring, sounding brisk and busy and not at all pleased at being bothered again.

She could hear the unmistakable sound of traffic in the background and knew she'd caught him on the road.

"It's Maddie," she said and let that little bit of news settle.

Judging by the tone of his voice, it didn't settle all that well. "Look," he said, forcing patience and what sounded like a reluctant form of contrition. "I'm really sorry I had to run out on you today."

"Twice," she reminded him because she just couldn't help herself.

"Yeah. Right. Twice. So I'm sorry twice. Can you just tell me what's on your mind? Is there a problem with the gallery, or what?"

"Or what," she said, took a breath, then took the plunge. "I'm pregnant. You're the father. I figured you should know. See ya."

When she hung up, her hands were shaking, her heart was pounding, and she'd turned as hot as the fire in her kiln.

For a moment all she could do was sit there. Then she made herself get up. She walked on wobbly legs to the bathroom then lost her lunch while the phone rang and rang and rang in the background.

Half an hour later she'd washed her face and drunk some herbal tea to settle her tummy. She was waiting on a customer when the gallery door burst open and one very large, very angry man stomped in.

"I damn near rear-ended a Toyota!"

Maddie's customer, a matronly woman wearing suede boots and high hair, turned from the piece of Raku she was considering as a Christmas gift for her niece. "I have a Toyota!" she cried and rushed toward the front window. "Tell me you didn't hit my Toyota!"

"You've got some nerve, hotshot!" Clay barked, ignoring the frazzled woman. Fists balled at his sides, his face red with cold and rage, he lurked in the midst of delicate pottery and fragile artwork looking for all the world like the proverbial bull in a china closet.

"I have a customer," Maddie hissed, keeping her voice low in the hopes of settling him down.

"I don't give a damn about your customer."

"But my Toyota!" the woman shrieked, lending another

level of anxiety to a tension strung as tight as the fit of his shirt stretched across his broad shoulders.

"Lady," Clay snapped as he spared the woman an impatient glance, raised his finger, then changed his mind. Stalking over to her, he firmly but politely took her arm and walked her directly to the door.

"We're closed," he growled and ushered her outside.

"Well, I never," she huffed as he slammed the door in her face, flipped the lock and turned around the Closed sign.

"What on earth do you think you're doing?" Maddie fumed, marching to the door and reaching for the lock.

"Leave it."

Telling herself she'd gone toe-to-toe with Clayton James too many times in her life to back down at this late date, she bristled right back at him. "You can't just waltz in here, scare off my customers and then close up my shop."

"In case you hadn't noticed, I'm a whole lot bigger than you, so I can do anything I damn well please," he roared, towering over her with a sneer so menacing she started backing away.

"And right now," he continued, dogging her every step of the way, "it would please me to wring your scrawny, little neck. How could you do that to me? How could you announce over the phone while I'm cruising down the highway at seventy miles per hour that we're going to have a baby and then hang up on me?"

She'd seen him angry before. But never like this. Never this pulse-pounding, eye-twitching, heat-radiating, ready-to-tear-something-apart-with-his-bare-hands rage that exploded from him like a rocket from a launch pad.

She wasn't easily intimidated though. She wasn't easily cowed. To make sure he understood that she would not be bullied, she did the one thing that neither of them expected her to do.

She drew a fortifying breath, touched a hand to her tummy—and threw up all over his boots.

It was a first, but he'd actually made a woman sick at the sight of him. And he was a little sick himself for the way he'd barged into her shop and bullied her.

There wasn't a name she could call him that Clay hadn't already called himself. He was an ogre. He was a bully. An insensitive, mean-spirited, bumbling fool.

But she hadn't called him a single one. For the first time in her life, this particular woman hadn't said a word.

Clay looked down with concern at Maddie's limp form. She'd been as light as a snowflake, as fragile as a piece of her pottery when he'd picked her up, carried her to her loft apartment and laid her down on her bed.

That had been a half hour ago. Since then, he'd pressed cold, wet compresses to her forehead, brought her soda crackers and tea. He'd cleaned up his boots and cleaned up her gallery floor. Through it all, the worst he'd had to endure was his worry and her silence.

As he sat at her side on the edge of the bed, he'd never felt so penitent in his life for what he'd put her through. Not just today—although that was bad enough—but for however long she'd known about the baby and had been dealing with it by herself.

Not that he hadn't done some suffering of his own the past few months. He'd been in the equivalent of hell since he'd left her in September. A day hadn't gone by that he hadn't wanted to go to her and tell her that he loved her, and beg her to take him on any terms she could dream up. A night hadn't passed when he hadn't ached to have her in his bed, in his arms, sighing his name in that breathless, shivery way that made him feel like no one or nothing mattered but him. He wanted to feel that way again.

And he was going to—just as soon as he convinced her

he was part of her life. And, he would, by God, be a big part of it from now on.

Keeping his distance had almost killed him. Well, from now on, distance wasn't going to be a factor in their relationship.

She may not love him, but that was tough. Even bullheaded women could be persuaded to change their minds. He was going to do everything in his power to make sure she had not only a change of mind but a change of heart. And he was going to start right now.

"Are you feeling better?" He placed a fresh compress on her forehead.

She let out a heavy breath. "You can quit hovering. I've made it this far. I don't need a nursemaid this late in the game."

Sympathy and guilt curled into a small, tight knot in his gut. "You've been sick a lot?"

She lifted a shoulder. "Goes with the territory. Besides— I'm pretty much over it."

"Yeah, I can see that," he muttered, feeling responsible and more determined by the moment that they were going to work this out.

It would help if she would look at him. The stubborn little gypsy just stared at the ceiling.

"Is everything okay? With the baby, I mean? With you?"

"Fine," she assured him wearily and slung a forearm over her eyes. "Everything's fine."

It was the strangest thing, this way he felt. Proprietary yet PO'd. Guilt jockeyed with joy. Pride wrestled with pain. And love—love hovered somewhere near hope.

"Why didn't you tell me?" he asked softly.

"I believe I just did."

"Sooner," he said, drawing on a newfound store of patience. "Why didn't you tell me sooner?"

She didn't have an answer for that, but he figured he did and he figured he'd just set her straight right now.

"We're in this together, Maddie."

Finally she looked at him. And finally, he understood.

"Did you really think I'd let you deal with this alone?"

Well, there it is, Maddie thought. The offer. The sacrifice. The noble James integrity strutting front and center to save the day. As much as she loved this man, she would not let him take her on as a charity case.

"I'm not asking for your help," she said as emphatically as her bruised heart would allow. "And I'm not expecting you to change your life. I just thought you had a right to know."

Her proclamation of independence was harder to voice than she'd expected.

He opened his mouth, closed it, opened it again. "You're not expecting me to change my life."

"That's right." She didn't want to think that he was feeling relief right now, but she figured he probably was. And while that knowledge cut deep and twisted, she made herself find the words to convince him she didn't want him in her life. "I want this baby, Clay. Its conception was an accident, and I'm sorry it involved you. But I'm not sorry about the baby. I'll always be grateful to you for your part in it, but I don't need or expect your help or participation."

He gave her a hard, unreadable stare. "I see. So I was just a convenient donor in all this, is that it?"

His anger was justifiable. She accepted that. What was hard to accept was how rapidly it escalated.

"How convenient for you that I was so accommodating. Well, guess what? You may not have any expectations, but I sure as hell do."

She eased up to her elbows as he bolted off the bed and paced to the other side of the room. He looked big and crowded and a little like a caged lion. Probably just how he feels, she thought, and barely avoided flinching when he rounded on her.

"You know, I may not have had as much time as you have to get used to this, and I sure as the world haven't had the chance to invest much thought in how it's going to impact my life. But I do know one thing—that baby is as much mine as it is yours and it's not going to grow up without a father."

She'd expected this obligatory response even as she'd hoped for something more. Something like, I love you, I love the idea of having a baby with you. She was still feeling the stinging absence of either when his next words rocked her back to the moment.

"You've got to the end of the day to pick a date, hot-shot."

"A date?" she parroted, a frisson of unease shivering down her spine as she watched him stalk toward the door.

"A wedding date," he clarified, stopping with one broad palm cupping the doorjamb. "Just make sure we get this done before Christmas."

"Get it done?" she repeated, as her own anger joined the fray and trotted right alongside of disbelief. "In the first place we're not talking about cooking a turkey here. In the second, I'm not marrying you."

"Before Christmas," he repeated with no room for fudging. "You set the date or I will."

And then he left. Without a backward glance. Without a word of love. Without a reason for her to believe he felt anything but obligation.

Eleven

"**F**or the last time, I'm not marrying anybody. And if I was, it wouldn't be you!" The connection was broken with a decisive crash.

"Hmm," Garrett said, as he listened, along with Clay, to the last message Maddie had left on Clay's answering machine. "It would seem you've got a problem."

"She's the one with the problem," Clay said, trying to camouflage a little self-pity with surliness. It had been three days since he'd found out about the baby and told Maddie to set a date. Since then he'd let the entire family in on the news and the impending wedding. "You'd think she'd be relieved that I told her I'd marry her."

Garrett stroked his jaw and eased a hip onto the corner of Clay's desk. "Told her? You mean, you didn't ask her?"

Clay shifted his shoulders, uncomfortable suddenly under Garrett's scrutiny. "Under the circumstances, it didn't seem necessary."

"Necessary," Garrett mused. "And I don't suppose you thought it was necessary to tell her you loved her, either."

Clay pressed a finger to a spot above his left eye, absently rubbed. "Love really doesn't have much to do with this," he hedged.

"Oh boy. Now I've heard it all. You're so in love with the woman you can't think straight." He held a hand in the air to stall Clay's objection. "Don't even try to deny it. You haven't been the same since Jesse and I collected the two of you from the cabin in the fall."

"I never have settled with you over that," Clay reminded his brother, thinking that now might be as good a time as any to shut Garrett up with a fist to his jaw.

"You don't really think you're fooling anyone do you?" Garrett went on, ignoring the dark look in Clay's eyes. "Anyone but Maddie, that is, and you've really done a number there. A woman is won with declarations of love not ultimatums. Think about it," he added on the way out the door. "And then do something about it."

Clay thought about it all right. He thought until his head hurt. And then he thought some more. It was in the middle of the night when those thoughts came together in a cohesive unit.

Finally it became as plain as the gold buckles on Jesse's rodeo belts. He'd just been too blinded by his own love to see it. That little gypsy loved him. Of course she loved him.

Hadn't she badgered and bristled and sniped at him exactly the way he'd badgered and bristled and sniped at her all these years? All these years that he'd loved her and just hadn't wanted to admit it? All these years that they'd both hidden their true feelings behind metaphorical barbwire fences, too stubborn and too afraid that the other one would find out? Just like him, she'd been hiding her vulnerability behind bristles because she'd been afraid she'd get hurt.

Lord what a pair.

A pair. He liked the sound of that. Suddenly he liked a lot of things that he hadn't been liking much of late. Like the sunrise. The sunsets. The prospect of a future with the wildest little bundle of sass and dazzle that a man could ever hope for. His heart swelled with pride at the thought of a son, then melted like chocolate at the image of a daughter who would have her mother's beautiful flashing eyes and sensitive artist's soul.

The trick was going to be convincing Maddie that he wanted not only her but the baby that came with the package.

In the Old West, a man could take what he wanted and the devil with anything else. He could ride into the night, steal his woman and make her his, whether she liked it or not.

But this wasn't the Old West. And Maddie Brannigan wasn't a woman who'd let even a semirespectable outlaw like him take her unless she wanted to be taken.

Nope. This wasn't the Old West. That didn't mean though, that he couldn't borrow a little from the past to get what he wanted.

By morning he had it all planned. He'd figured out exactly how he was going to make her see what it had taken him too many years and too many sleepless nights to see for himself.

Wildflowers. Hundreds of them. They'd been arriving since ten o'clock Monday morning and they just kept coming. Maddie had filled vases and glasses and buckets and still they came.

Even as she scowled at the outrageous splashes of color and scents, her heart turned as mushy as an overripe peach. The man played dirty. He played on secret fantasies that she'd been stupid enough to share.

Committed to being angry instead of swayed by his extravagant gesture, she grabbed the phone and dialed.

When she finally connected with Clay, she practically barked into the mouthpiece. "I want this to stop."

"You don't like the flowers?" he asked, as sweet as a pecan pie at a Christmas potluck.

She loved the flowers. She loved the smile in his voice, the charm of the gesture. But she refused to be fooled, just like she refused to marry him for the wrong reasons. He didn't love her. He was just doing the honorable thing.

"I know what you're doing and it's not going to work," she informed him, standing in the middle of her gallery, surrounded by color and springtime and hounded by a niggling, romantic little voice that whispered ridiculous notions in her ear. Notions like, maybe he cares about you after all. Maybe you should stop and think this over.

Then there was his voice to contend with. The one that whispered across the line and made her knees go as mushy as her heart. "Marry me, Maddie."

His words warmed her like the tummy-tingling burn of rich brandy. Made her think of midnight kisses and slow, sensual hands.

"It's not going to happen," she informed him shakily, and wished she sounded more convincing. "So you can just take your misguided notions of obligation and responsibility and peddle them somewhere else. I do not need you to marry me, so don't bother trying to convince me that it's what you want to do." While she still had the strength of will to do it, she slammed down the receiver and disconnected him from her life.

Hugging an arm around her slightly expanding waistline, she wrapped her fingers tighter around the gold coin that she carried with her everywhere she went and tried to remember why this was the hill she'd chosen to die on.

* * *

The boxes arrived the next day. Dozens of them.

"What is this? I didn't order this," she insisted as the UPS man diligently unloaded carton after carton of glazing compound from her favorite supplier in Missouri.

"Just sign here," he said, pushing a clipboard and a shipping slip under her nose.

"But I didn't order this. And I can't pay for it. Not this much."

He thumbed back his cap and checked the slip. "It's all paid for, so I guess there's no problem. Please, lady, just sign. I've got a bizillion more packages to deliver yet today, and the wife's having her sister for dinner. Do I have to tell you how much heat I'll take if I'm late?"

In a bit of a daze she signed the receipt.

And then a small smile won the battle with her scowl and crept like a mountain sunrise across her face.

She turned a circle around the boxes, slowly made her way to the phone when it began to ring.

"Necessities," she answered, mentally tallying up the phenomenal cost of the precious glazes that were fundamental to her Raku.

"Marry me," drifted over the line like a golden, glorious caress.

She gripped the receiver with both hands, bit back tears that could have been fear, or joy, or glimmers of both. Without a word, she slowly replaced the receiver in its cradle.

Then she sat down in the middle of the floor, tugged a disgruntled Maxwell onto her lap and bawled like a baby.

Christmas Eve day dawned crisp and cold. Winter sunlight streamed through the windows of Necessities, glancing off intricate pieces of stained glass, dancing across tapestries and setting a selection of Raku glistening.

Business had been brisk all day. Last-minute shoppers

had turned out in droves with fat wallets and phenomenal credit limits. Spirits were high. So were Maddie's sales.

It was already dark when she finally closed the doors to the shop at five o'clock. She was exhausted and feeling just a tad melancholy that the holidays were almost over.

Because of Savannah's and Ryan's demanding schedules, the family had decided to celebrate Christmas on the weekend after the actual holiday. While it made sense and was a practical solution for their annual dilemma, Maddie found herself feeling very alone on the eve of this holiday that above all others represented harmony and unity and love for their fellow man.

Oh, well, she thought. She and Maxwell would share a bowl of popcorn, watch "It's a Wonderful Life" and then toddle off to bed.

She'd just placed the Closed sign in the door and had pulled the shade when she heard the jingle of sleigh bells.

She had too much of the child in her to resist a peek outside. A nearby streetlamp spotlighted snow that drifted like diamond dust to the ground and accumulated in fluffy garlands on sidewalk benches draped with evergreen boughs.

The jingling grew louder. Any moment now she expected to see sweet Mr. Ludwig round the corner in his sleigh. Every year he dressed up like Santa and decked out his old sorrel gelding, Topper, with reindeer antlers. Together they would treat the town to the sight of them prancing around the square.

But she didn't see Mr. Ludwig and Topper. What she saw instead had her blinking her eyes then opening her door. Oblivious to the fact that she was dressed only in a lacy white Western-cut dress that was her traditional Christmas Eve day outfit, she stepped outside to get a better look.

In rapt fascination she watched as a midnight-black stallion, trimmed in an ornate harness of tooled leather and polished chrome and pulling a sleek two-seater sleigh, danced down the street in her direction. The sleigh bells draped over the magnificent animal's withers rang into the twilight like delicate chimes as the sleigh, as richly appointed as the harness and lined with tufted crimson velvet, slid to a graceful stop in front of her door.

And the man—the man who uttered a soft "Whoa" then looped the reins over the brake—was watching her face like he expected her to run at the first utterance of the *M* word.

Dressed in a black, Western-cut suit beneath a heavy herringbone dress coat, he swung gracefully down from the cutter, settled his coal-black Stetson more firmly on his head, then walked unerringly toward her.

She'd seen more beautiful sights. At the moment she couldn't remember when—not all that unusual considering she couldn't even remember her name.

His blue eyes glistened in the lamplight. His breath feathered out like crystal fog, melding with the steady fall of snow. And the slightly frosted bouquet of flowers he placed in her trembling hands were as alive with color as the reckless rhythm of her wildly beating heart.

"Fool woman," he said softly as he shrugged out of his coat and bundled it around her shoulders. "You don't have the sense to stay in out of the cold, do you?"

On another day, in another time, she'd have fired an answering volley back at him. But tonight his gentle admonishment didn't feel like a criticism. It felt like a caress. Like a promise that if she didn't have the sense to take care of herself he'd be there to do it for her.

The cold ache of loneliness that had enveloped her heart for too long melted to a warm, tender glow.

"The horse was dirty pool, James. And the sleigh—" Her lower lip quivered and she batted back tears. "I'll never forgive you for that."

Clay had expected resistance. His heart expanded with love for the valiant effort she made. When she went a little pale, he bracketed her shoulders with his hands and bent down so his face was on a level with hers. "You're not going to get sick again, are you?"

She pinched her lips together and gave her head a rebellious little shake.

"You're going to cry, though, aren't you?"

She nodded helplessly as a renegade tear trickled down her cheek.

"Emma warned me that this might happen," he murmured against her hair as he folded her protectively into his warmth and marveled at the depth of his love. "I was hoping maybe you'd hold off until after I asked the question."

"Don't you dare," she demanded in a muffled plea somewhere in the vicinity of his neck. "Don't you dare ask me to marry you."

He hugged her hard and long. "Maddie, Maddie. What am I going to do with you?"

"Just leave me alone."

"Sorry, hotshot. No can do."

She struggled through a shaky sigh.

"Come," he urged gently. "Just come with me."

When she said nothing, he pressed his advantage, tucked her under his arm and walked her toward the cutter. After he'd carefully assisted her onto the velvet seat, he covered her with a lap blanket then climbed up beside her.

A soft slap of reins on the stallion's hind quarters set the sleigh in motion with a shush of snow and a rich jingle of bells.

As they glided along snow-packed streets toward the other end of town, she finally began to suspect what he had in mind. "We'd better not be going where I think we're going."

He only smiled.

The church. He was taking her to the church! The rapid-fire beat of her heart told her there was more than an early Christmas Eve worship service on the agenda.

And as he eased to a skillful stop in a spot left between a half a dozen cars—cars that she recognized as Garrett and Emma's, Maya and Logan's...cars with California license plates that could only belong to her brother and sister and her parents...and a pickup with Wyoming plates and rodeo gear in the back rounded out the lot—she knew that Reverend Considine was waiting inside, primed and ready to deliver a wedding ceremony.

"This is so like you!" she snapped refusing to step out of the cutter when he raised his hands to lift her down. "You've got everything all figured out, all planned out nice and neat and tidy." Oblivious to her wilting bouquet, she gripped the lap blanket tighter between her fingers when he tried to eased it away. "Well it's not you know. Life isn't neat and tidy, and it doesn't always go your way, Clayton James."

"Life hasn't gone my way since I left you at your apartment in September," he said, giving up the fight over the blanket and earnestly meeting her eyes.

She refused to look at him. "You couldn't wait to get rid of me."

"Wrong. I couldn't wait to get away from you. There's a difference."

When she slanted him a questioning look, he folded her cold fingers in his. "I couldn't wait to get away from you because I couldn't stand to be around you, loving you the way I do and knowing you didn't love me back."

"Not love you?" she blurted out, then caught her lower lip between her teeth when she realized what she'd just admitted.

He grinned and felt his heart swell. "You're quite a woman, Matilda Brannigan."

"But not your *ideal* woman," she sputtered with a bite of sarcasm.

"Nope. Definitely not my ideal," he agreed, and touched a hand to her cheek to brush away a fluff of snow. "You're wild and reckless and impulsive. You're militantly independent and just about as soothing to a man's soul as sandpaper on a blister."

When she turned her soulful eyes down to him, he gently pried her fingers from the blanket and lifted her to the ground. "Half the time I don't know whether I want to kiss you or spank you. But all the time," he continued, cupping her cheeks in his hands and with the slight pressure of his thumbs under her chin, tipping her face to his, "all the time, I can't imagine spending the rest of my life without you."

Her eyes glittered, a beautiful competition for the sparkling dance of the falling snow.

"It scares me to death when I think of the havoc you're going to wreak on my nice, ordered life," he said lovingly, "but it scares me more to think of living that life without you."

She closed her eyes, warmed by the caress of his.

"Can I ask you that question now, Maddie?"

Complacent suddenly, and subtly, joyfully coy, she blinked into his eyes. "Which question would that be?"

If his heart beat any harder, he wouldn't be able to hear himself talk. "The one that goes like this. Will you marry me? Will you marry me because I love you, and I can't stand the thought of not arguing or fighting or being irritated with you for the rest of my life? Will you marry me because you love me?"

She sniffed, let out a quivering little breath. "That's three questions."

He shook his head, smiled. "Then you got a bargain, sweetheart, because I only need one answer."

She gave it to him. With her eyes, with her smile, with the one simple word that told him of the love she'd never hide from him again. "Yes."

Ten minutes later, with their family watching misty-eyed, Mad Dog Brannigan became Mrs. Banana Boy James.

An hour after that he had her tucked naked in his bed where he'd wanted her since what seemed like forever.

And one blissful hour after that, he shut her sweet, sassy mouth with a kiss to stall their first argument as man and wife over what they were going to name the baby.

* * * * *

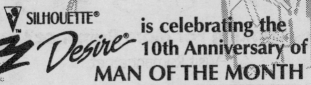
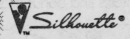

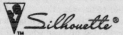

COMING NEXT MONTH

#1189 BELOVED—Diana Palmer
Long, Tall Texans
Beguiling Tira Beck had secretly saved herself for Simon Hart, January's *10th Anniversary Man of the Month*. But this long, tall Texan wouldn't give beautiful Tira the time of day. And she wasn't about to surrender her *nights* to the stubborn-but-irresistible bachelor…unless he became her beloved!

#1190 THE HONOR BOUND GROOM—Jennifer Greene
Fortune's Children: The Brides
His prestigious name was the *only* thing formidable businessman Mac Fortune was offering pregnant, penniless Kelly Sinclair. But once this dutiful groom agreed to honor sweet Kelly, would he love and cherish her, too?

#1191 THE BABY CONSULTANT—Anne Marie Winston
Butler County Brides
Father-by-default Jack Ferris desperately needed instruction in baby-care basics. And Frannie Brooks was every toddler's—and **every** virile man's—dream. Now, if Jack could only convince the sexy consultant to care for his child…and to help him make a few of their own!

#1192 THE COWBOY'S SEDUCTIVE PROPOSAL—Sara Orwig
A simple "yes" to Jared Whitewolf's outrageous proposal and Faith Kolanko would have her dream: a home *and* a baby. But she wanted a husband, too, not some heartbreaker in a ten-gallon hat. Could a ready-made marriage turn this reckless cowboy into a straight-'n'-narrow spouse and father?

#1193 HART'S BABY—Christy Lockhart
Zach Hart wasn't about to open his ranch to sultry stranger Cassie Morrison just because he and her baby shared a strong family resemblance. He had to beware of fortune seekers…and their adorable, chubby-cheeked children! Then again, what could it hurt if they stayed just *one* night…?

#1194 THE SCANDALOUS HEIRESS—Kathryn Taylor
Was the diner waitress really a long-lost heiress? Clayton Reese had fallen so deeply for the down-to-earth beauty that he wasn't sure if Mikki Finnley was born into denim or diamonds. This lovestruck lone wolf had no choice but to find the truth…and follow his heart wherever it might lead.